Unau Arrangements

Viiola May

Copyright © 2012 Viiola may

There is no growth without change and there is no change without loss - Rick Warren

ASTRID AND DARIAN'S PLAYLIST!

yam yam: No Vacation

Black dog: Arlo Parks

Pretty When You Cry: Lana Del Ray

Be OK: Ingrid Michaelson

Love In The Sky:The Weeknd

Lady In Spain: Ingrid Michaelson

I'm Sorry I Made You Cry:
Connie Francis

That Funny Feeling: Phoebe
Bridgers

Blouse: Clairo

SUPERPOSITION:Daniel Caesar,
John Mayor

Poison: Rita Ora

CHAPTER ONE

"So, what'd you think? Not too shabby, huh?" My dad says as I look around at my surroundings seeing the light blue cotton sofa and wooden rustic coffee table.

It's not really my style, if I'm being honest.

"Boy, do I have some memories in this place" My dad chirps out whilst smiling at me and Eli as I look around at the large beach house.

"It's not home." I announce and my father puts his head in his hands sitting down on the sofa like I'd just ripped a piece of his heart out.

"I've already told you hundreds of times Astrid it was your mother's decision to finalise the divorce when we get home things are going to change, this summer is one last chance to be carefree god Astrid be a teenage make friends, I don't want to see you in your room writing in that stupid journal of yours!" My father says as I glare at him.

"Mum would've never finalised the divorce if you never cheat......." I start to say as I stop myself and look at my father feeling guilt hit me like a ton of bricks.

"Yea dad I will have fun, make friends and do whatever." I say robotically as I fake a smile at my father giving him the sliver of hope that he craves.

"That's my girl." He mumbles attempting to sound like a father as Eli smirks at me.

"I'm glad you said that because a couple friends from band camp want me to come to a kickback tonight, I said you'd tag along!" Eli announces walking out onto the ocean view decking as I follow him.

"And what friend is that huh? I don't remember you ever having friends." I say smugly digging at him.

"well, there's Aaron, Wes and Darian." Eli answers me as I laugh at him.

"Darian?" I ask looking at my brother smiling sweetly.

"Yeah, do you know him or something?" Eli questions looking suspiciously convinced as I laugh.

"No, I'm just surprised you know guys with such stupid ass names!" I say mockingly, smirking at my brother as he hits my arm and I yelp.

"Like Astrid's a normal name!" Eli says smirking and crossing his arms.

"Like Astrid's a Bla Bla Bla." I say mockingly sticking my tongue out.

"Just get ready for nine, okay?" Eli says as he starts to walk back into the house before I get a chance to answer. He waits at the door and turns around to face me. I take it as my chance to make a sly dig.

"I mean if I have to ass face, I guess I will!" I shout after him as he rolls his eyes and shouts back.

"You do have too!"

"Oh goodie!" I say taking my dark blue converse off and dipping my feet into the ocean, shivering feeling the cold wave hit my toes.

The time hits nine and I run out into the living room shuffling through boxes and boxes. I am looking for my black leather jacket to pair with my black skinny jeans and grey cropped vest top.

Once I find it I run out the front door. I notice Eli is standing waiting for me wearing a Hawaiian shirt and a pair of light blue swimming trunks. My eyes skim over him as I hold back an evil cackle.

"Do you have to look like such a doofus!" I say glaring at Him as he glares back at me looking rather piqued by my curtness.

"And do you always have to talk like such a naive little child? Oh wait you are nineteen what should I expect?" Eli retorts as I roll my eyes.

"Oh, I forgot, you were born two years before me you are so old dude, so are we heading out or is the party starting at the front door? I think I hear the music!" I say mockingly as he mimics me but starts to walk. I follow not far behind him.

As I walk, feeling my short legs aching, I complain, "How long?".

"Eli......" I murmur and he ignores me.

"I'm tired Eli." I complain as he looks back at me and rolls his eyes exasperated by my tired pleas.

"We've been walking five minutes, quit complaining." Eli says glaring at me as I roll my eyes. I look in front of us and see a group of guys and a couple of girls.

"Can I leave now, please?" I question feeling my social anxiety prickling my stomach.

"No, you can't, but look at that girl she's smiling so go mingle maybe get her number for me!" Eli says pushing me forward a bit too enthusiastically because I stumble forward landing in the sand underneath me as I turn and glare at him.

"Oops at least now you look a little less stiff!" He says smirking as I stand up and brush off the sand on my Jeans.

"Darian my guy!" Eli says to some guy sitting behind a tree up a table sniffing God knows what.

"Eli its good to see you again man, come have a line." That Darian guy says smirking as he stands up and hugs Eli, he then looks at me then sits back down. I glare at him then turn around and start to mumble about how much I hate parties.

"Astrid what are you doing just standing there? Can you get that chick's number for me and quit looking so depressed!" Eli shouts as I turn and scowl at him.

"This isn't my scene, drugs aren't my thing and I don't ever remember them being yours Either wannabe pill popper." I snap as that Darian guy looks up at me and smirks. I just roll my eyes.

"You too good for this huh, pretty girl?" He asks lowly as I glare at him.

"Yeah, I am and what about it." I snap crossing my arms. I turn away from them both feeling bored.

I walk over to the girl smiling at me.

"Hey I'm Astrid my brother wants to know if you're single." I say smiling at the girl as my wavy dark brown hair blows in my face. I take a hair tie off my wrist and tie my messy hair back.

"Hey I'm Elle and no I'm dating Aaron. You see that guy? Yeah, the one chugging the beer upside down, that's him." She says as I nod.

"Good to know, sorry my brother would have bugged me all night.. I figured I might as well bite the bullet and see if you were interested. Now I know that you're not I can walk over to him and gloat in his stupid face." I say smiling as I turn around looking at my brother as he waves and I smirk sticking my middle finger up.

"I get it, my brother's the same, so you just moved here." Elle smiles, pushing her red hair out of her face as it blows against the wind.

"For the summer only, then I'm off to college." I say feeling bitter towards my father for making me leave my mother.

"Oh, cool we go surfing every Saturday. You should totally come with your brother too!" She says smiling as I nod reluctantly.

"Yes, sure I mean if my asshole brother wants to" I say as she laughs.

CHAPTER TWO

"Yes, Astrid I want to do some surfing."
Someone says grabbing my shoulder making
me jump. I swing round on my heel and see
that it's Eli standing next to Druggy, I mean
Darian.

"Hey why did you have to make me jump like
that?" I snap hitting Eli in the balls abruptly.

"Ouch you bitch!" He snaps stumbling a few
steps as I smile at him. I look round and
notice Darian smiling at me. I turn to him,
smile then stick my middle finger up.

"So, we should dance!" Elle says smiling and
before I get a chance to agree or disagree she
pulls my hand to dance with her.

I'm dancing to drunk in love by Beyonce with Elle as we move our hands down our bodies and roll our hips to the music.

"Eww my brother won't stop staring at you! "Elle shouts over the music as I look over at the dark haired druggy who's stood watching me whilst smirking.

I turn away from Elle and start walking toward him.

I notice Darian still staring at me as I glare at him but he doesn't move, he just stays looking at me intensely. Weirdo.

"Quit staring cokehead!" I snap as I glare at him and he laughs deeply in an intimidating masculine way.

"Stop dancing like a Slut then." He shouts over the music as I turn around and smirk.

"I'll show you slut!" I hiss out as I walk up to one of the guys Eli's been hanging out with and I start to dance with him. I grind up and down him as I watch Darian. He walks up to us abruptly, pushing me out of the way. He punches the guy in the mouth as I stare in horror.

"What the hell you dick, I was dancing!" I shout standing in front of Darian hitting his chest as everyone starts to fight. I try to see if the guy is okay but Darian pulls my hand and leads me away from everyone.

"You are fucking nuts, creep!" I hissed, glaring at him as he laughed.

He pulls me close to him as I look at him in his dilated eyes.

"No one talks to me like that!" He shouts as I push him back with the palm of my hands.

"Then maybe they should." I snap as he grins.

"Let me take you out, we'd be good together" He says huskily as I put my finger on my chin pretending to think.

"Ugh well let's see, no." I say smirking as I walk away and he calls after me.

"You will go out with me Astrid!" He shouts.

"Never going to happen not even in your dreams, cokehead!" I shout back sticking my middle finger up at him as he laughed smugly.

"What was that about?" Elle asks as I laugh.

"Not a clue!" I say honestly, since I had no idea what just happened. It felt like a fever dream.

I walk over to my brother tapping his shoulder as he makes out with some girl.

"God Eli I'm tired I want to go home!" I say complaining as he flaps his hand at me motioning for me to leave him alone.

"It's getting dark Eli, I want to go to bed!" I whinge.

"Go then!" He hisses and pushes me back as I glare at him.

"Screw you asshole!" I snap as I walk away with my hands in my pocket.

I pull my phone out as everyone continues to drink and dance.

"Hello dad I think something's wrong with Eli. He's been sniffing something white and now he's on the floor and his eyes are really wide." I say down the phone as I look over and glare at my brother who's still making out with the girl.

"Don't worry sweetie don't be scared I'm about to call the police now, you were right we are heading home tonight!" He says as I smile to myself.

"To stay with mum?" I inquire, hoping to see my mother.

"Yes, if that's what you want, you can stay with her!" Dad says as I can hear him talk through gritted teeth.

"It is." I say quietly.

"Okay, I'm on my way. Be sure to look after your brother." my father says with concern to his tone.

"I knew bringing you kids here would be a foolish idea. I just wanted us to have one last summer together." He says down the phone as I sit on the curb with my knees up.

"We can try again next summer, theres always next summer." I tell him trying to give him hope that for once things will be normal in our family.

As the cold night wind breezes through the air I hold my knees and rub my hands against them for warmth as he says, "Yeah, maybe next summer."

CHAPTER THREE

DEAR FUCKED UP THOUGHT VENT

My father is a liar.

I won't be spending next summer with my father because as soon as the phone call ended, he dropped us off home and left he didn't even come in the house.

A week later I got a Facebook message from his associate assistant Susan saying.

"Your father loves you Astrid, and Eli so much with his whole heart but he had to leave he couldn't be held down anymore. He has feelings for me and we are in love. He will come back when you and your brother aren't angry anymore. He's left your mother with enough money to move closer to your college so you don't have to pay for on campus residency. I know Astrid it's difficult for you to comprehend at such a young age. Please step out of your shoes and put yourself in your father's shoes.

Sincerely Susan.

OH FUCK YOU SUSAN.

How about that!

As a result, my father cheated on my mother with said Susan, and my mother is now on her own with me, Eli, and our two-year-old brother bear.

Anyway, rant adverted, we are moving, in a couple of days. In the midst of packing up all my stuff and throwing out items I've kept since childhood, I'm grieving my childhood

home while experiencing an unbearable guilt.
I feel like I've just discarded a vital organ.
In terms of getting rid of clutter, I have
already thrown out two big black bags of
miscellaneous items.

My mother said Eli was allowed to live at
home with us during his first year at ELAC;
however, he insisted on living on campus to
become one of those annoying ass frat boys,
lecturing on a tandem about how imperative it
is to make frat brothers because they are for
life.

Eleven Hilgard Avenue here we come.

The reason I stuff my thick leather journal
under my mattress is because if I don't, Eli
will find it and see all my crazy mental
thoughts.

When I walked downstairs, I found bear watching SpongeBob on the couch and my mother preparing dinner. Standing at the kitchen counter, I grab a carrot off of the chopping board. Sitting on the stool, I take a big bite into it while leaning over to see what my mother is doing.

"Are you still fine with watching Bear tonight? I have a double shift until 6 a.m." my mother asks as she glances at me through tired eyes. I nod in agreement.

"It's not like I have a social life anyway." My mother looks at me sympathetically as I shrug. Oh boy, here we go!

"Sweetie what happened to Elle? He umm he told me you two really hit it off!"My mother says. She refuses to say my father's name or even acknowledge him. This has been a new habit of my mothers since my father left, I can't blame her I don't mention his name much anymore either.

"She's moved to London to attend Harvard. We don't talk much because of the distance" I mutter as I acknowledge covetousness in my stomach and I try to mute it.

After rejection from Harvard and barely getting into UCLA, it was thanks to the assistance I received from my father that I was accepted. I wish I had never had that as it's something he can always hold onto and say, "Well Astrid I got you into UCLA you owe me." Besides, I hate owing people things. My preferred course of action would be to wait a long time and to do something on my own without the need for assistance from others. However, I received what I was given.

But hey it's too late now.

My father is an attorney, a hell of a competent one.. I hate to admit it, but he might be one of the most accomplished lawyers in the state. That's how I got into UCLA. After pleading John Reinheimer's case, he was released from custody and allowed to go home. He also won the case over a robbery he had committed whilst drunk after a filthy, drunken night at a strip club.

Therefore, John Reinheimer owed my father a favour. It was like he was making a deal with the devil. The devil being my father.

Anyway, John managed to get me into UCLA adding most extracurricular activities to my high school resume. However, I never actually achieved any. I tried a bunch. Let's just say I had a short attention span. Whenever I was excited about something the excitement would leave as fast as it came. However, the UCLA school board doesn't need to know that.

"Wow, her mum must be so proud of her!" My mother says awestruck as I nod reluctantly.

"Well, I wouldn't know!" I say bitterly knowing Elle ditched me when she found out it was me who squealed at the summer beach party. It was never me who called the police it was my father but still, I was to blame.

"It's okay sweetheart you will make new friends and hey your Big Twentieth birthday is coming up in a couple of months!" My mother says excitedly as she chops red and yellow peppers for dinner.

"Yes, twenty just another reminder that I'm one year closer to death." I say sarcastically as I chomp on a carrot.

"Don't speak like that around your brother please and try to be a little more optimistic and positive if you do that watch people want to be around you all the time!" My mother says stroking my cheek as I roll my eyes.

"Right thanks for the pep talk mum!" I say smiling a small smile as she nods.

"Anytime sweetheart." She says smiling, showing small frown lines on her forehead.

Often my mother likes to pretend she is fine through the day because she is a nurse so most of the time, she is working. Anyway, this does not stop me from hearing her sobbing in bed from time to time. I don't venture in because I do not want to intrude on her privacy, and I know that when I cry a lot, no one cares enough to listen. So, I listen to her through the wall as she weeps.

CHAPTER FOUR

"Hey be careful with that, that stuff is valuable you know!" I hiss feeling infuriated with the dumb mindless moving guy as he lifts one of my heavy boxes full of mementos from my life.

I walk into the newly built house with Bear in my arms as I balance him on my right hip whilst looking around the house.

Admittedly it is huge and a lot roomier than the old house. I have the option of three rooms since my brother no longer lives with us but it's not home yet, it doesn't feel like it is.

I walk upstairs and walk to the second closest room to the stair case.

"This is my room" I say out loud in an announcement to no one but myself. I walk in with Bear balanced on my hip.

The bedroom is just plain white with white curtains that have black flowers on. The previous owners must've left them but they're pretty so I guess they can stay.

I pull the curtain back peering out the window. It's not much of a view. My window is facing directly to next door's window. In fact I can see a bedroom that looks like a guy's one because the walls are a dark shade of olive green but the light is red.

Umm okay strange.

I put Bear down on the floor and take a closer look out of the window.

Oh my god.

An inundation of trepidation flows through me, Ahh.

It's Darian and some blonde girl. I watch her bounce up and down on top of him on top of his bed or what I can make out is a bed. The blonde hair of the girl flows down her back as she bounces up and down. I quickly close the curtains and put my hand over my eyes as I groan out loudly.

Ughhhhhhhhhhhhhhhh

I pick Bear up and walk downstairs as mum is handing the delivery man some cash. He glares at me as he makes his way out. I push my head forward like a rooster trying to be intimidating but he just chuckles and leaves.

"Mum I think, I don't think we can move here, there's well there's really nasty damp and it's shitty and!"I start to say trying to find any excuse as I panic the memory of the mini live porno I just saw flashes through my mind. My mother interrupts me.

"Bear should not hear that language how many times Astrid, and it's too late to change the location." It's here or on campus and we can't afford campus at the moment so realistically this is our only option. I think it's perfect for a small family like ours." My mother says as I get ready to argue but notice my mother's phone starts to ring.

"I've just worked a twelve-hour shift and moved house. Can I please have the night off? I know I need the money but I can't work again!"My mother says to her boss abruptly standing up for herself as I smile.

That's my mother. Go her.

"I know I know, no it's fine I can come in!" My mother says as I sigh loudly.

She puts the phone down and tries to speak but I interrupt this time.

"I know, I know I got to watch Bear and make dinner and put him to bed!" I say as she nods, she walks over to me and kisses my cheek.

"I promise I will make it up to you" she says and I shake my head.

"You don't need to!" I say hugging her.

An hour later my mother is at work. The pasta bake I made is in the oven and Bear is on the sofa watching cartoons whilst I unpack more stuff from the kitchenware box.

There's a knock at the front door. I walk up to the door and look through the peep hole before opening it because I'm concerned about stranger danger.

"Oh my god!" I say feeling mortified as I glance through the peephole once again. Darian is standing outside waiting for me to open the door. I wonder if he saw me watching earlier. I wasn't watching, I just saw what was happening and observed for a second.

Fuck, this is a disaster.

I sigh a deep breath and open the front door.

"Hi" I say looking up at him as his welcoming smile turns to a soul shattering glare.

"What the hell, no one told me a rat was moving in next door!" He says glaring at me.

"What'd you want Cokehead? I'm not interested in buying drugs!" I hiss out as he focuses on my brother.

"Well, Well the rat has a child!" He says smirking as I glare at him.

"That's strange actually because when I met you my gut feeling told me you were a virgin and well it's never wrong but maybe this time it is!" He says smirking as heavy blotches of red mantle my cheeks.

"What do you want?" I query as he laughs a deep unsettling laugh.

"Well, my father sent me over to welcome the newly arrived neighbours but since it's you I thought you should know while you are living next to me as long as I see you and I am around you, I will make your life a living hell and that's a promise!" He promises with undoubted certainty and I gulp then shake my head.

"And why would I care! "I say huffing out my lips and crossing my arms as he walks closer to me till I'm stopped between him and the kitchen counter.

I look up at him in his ocean blue eyes and watch as a large grin makes its way to his mouth and takes centre stage on his face.

He slowly leans over almost like in slow motion and whispers in my ear sending a chill right down my back.

"You'll see!" He says and then turns around shoves his hands in his pockets and walks out of the house.

CHAPTER FIVE

DEAR FUCKED UP THOUGHT VENT

Today is my first day at UCLA. I leave in about 10 minutes. I'm worried, at my old school I didn't fit in. At the school before that I didn't fit in either. I was often the target of bullies calling me nasty names like bummed out bitch and short fat troll.

I never really cared though because who decides what gets to me or not?

I do and it didn't get to me, I wouldn't let it.

But now Dad is gone things are different, things are getting to me more. I feel like I'm on the thin line of breaking. Hopefully I don't, hopefully I stay vigilant to losing my cool.

"Astrid it's time to head out!" my mum shouts up the stairs to me. I stuff my journal away and sprint downstairs.

"Oh, sweetie you look lovely!" My mother says as I look at her in confusion.

I'm wearing an old navy-blue T-shirt with writing saying LA heart and a pair of low waisted skinny Levi dark blue jeans. I don't look lovely, I look regular.

I just shrugged and accepted the compliment because what's the point in analyzing it, because it was sweet of her.

Even if it wasn't 100% true.

What's that saying that you always look perfect from your mother's eye line?

Well, there is some truth to that.

"Are you still okay to pick your brother up from nursery after college? "My mother asks as I nod.

"Okay let's go. "My mother announces holding Bear in her arms and walking out the front door. I grab my backpack off the stairs and run out the front door after her.

Once I arrive outside of campus, I look up to the sky in hopes for some sort of a sign that it's going to be a good day. The sign doesn't appear, of course.

I'm walking and texting away to my brother asking him how he is doing at his first internship at some fancy tech store.

I feel a large broad chest bump into my considerably smaller one. I stumbled back onto the floor my books tumbling out of my bag spilling everywhere. A tampon slides right out of my bag across the hall.

"Oh my god." I murmur as I widen my eyes.

"This yours?" A deep voice echoes and I feel a chill up my spine. I look up and it's Darian.

My cheeks glow a florescent shade of rose pink and I nod standing up.

He leans into me as I look up at him my hands tremendously clammy as I take the tampon from his grasp.

"Watch where you're walking next time specs!" He hisses pushing me forward as I fall back down onto the floor picking up my books. He walks off and I'm trying to get all my stuff together as the bell tolls. I sigh feeling defeated because I know I'm probably going to be late for my first class.

"Here let me help!" A tall boy with pale blonde hair wearing a pink shirt says. He looks at me with a welcoming smile.

"Thanks, I'm so late!" I say in a panic.

"What are you majoring in?" the boy asks softly as I pull out my timetable.

"English literature." I say as he nods.

"Good we have the same classes let me walk with you, I'm Seth and from now on we are best friends " he says smiling whilst holding out his hand for me to shake and I nod and take his hand shaking it whilst juggling my bag and books in my free hand.

"Yes, I'm Astrid, it's good to meet you!" I say smiling at him awkwardly as we walk to class.

"Oh, by the way don't make eye contact with Erin!" Seth announces killing the silence as I look at him in confusion.

"Why?" I ask confused by his perceptive comment.

"Oh, she thinks she's the shit, she's not!" Seth says pushing his blonde meandering hair out of his eyes.

"You aren't a fan?" I ask looking up at him as he shakes his head.

"We've been sworn enemies since like kindergarten. I decided to come out the closet and she didn't like it because it took the spotlight off of her!" Seth says as I can't help but snigger at his dramatic point.

"I think she sucks, most people do!" I say honestly and cynically as he nods.

"See I knew we'd be friends!" Seth exclaims as I laugh.

Two hours later.

"So which ones Erin?" I ask as we take our lunches to an empty table.

"You see the blonde sitting on the tall black haired hunk's lap? That's her!" Seth says as I look over to where he's pointing and my cheeks flush red.

"Oh my god!" I murmur.

"What, do you know her?" Seth questions raising his eyebrow and looking at me confused as I shake my head and Audrey walks up to our table and sits down.

Audrey is tall and has emerald-green eyes and ginger hair. She's pretty, she's the kind of pretty that knows it but doesn't take advantage of it like Erin.

"He's my neighbour I saw them last night you know super close together." I say as her eyes widen and Seth laughs.

"You saw them fucking!" Audrey says out loud. Her voice echoes off the lunch hall walls as everyone's eyes dart to us and my cheeks heat rapidly.

"Audrey!" I hiss as I turn and watch Darian walk up to us.

"God Darian is so dreamy!" Seth says putting his hand on his chin in a dreamlike state and I roll my eyes.

"Who'd you watch fucking?" Darian asks as I look down at the floor and he pulls me up out of my seat by my arm and my eyes meet his.

"Who'd you see fucking Astrid?" He whispers, his voice dark and cold like a glacier.

"You" I murmur but he doesn't hear me as I mentally face palm.

"Well did you enjoy it?" he asks with a mischievous smirk playing on his lips.

I shake my head fast.

"No." I hiss out glaring at him feeling my hackles rising.

"Who'd you see fucking, huh specs?" He shouts as everyone's eyes are on us.

So much for being invisible to the public eye.

I push my glasses up my face and shake my head.

"No one now get off me, you big lump!" I say trying to pry my hand out of his grasp.

"Specs here likes to watch people fucking, don't you?" Darian says laughing as the lunch hall erupts with erratic spells of laughter and I gulp, Seth and Audrey watch me with apologetic eyes.

He lets go of me and I scatter out the lunch hall.

CHAPTER SIX

DEAR FUCKED UP THOUGHT VENT

Why am I so cynical? I mean why not? It's who I am, aren't I?

Why is happy and joy even an emotion? I haven't felt those feelings in a long time. I wonder what it's like to be one of those average Joes who is effortlessly happy and smiley all the time. I wonder what it's like to not have a care in the world like I wouldn't give a fuck if my mother makes a dig about my weight or my annoying ass neighbour who keeps having parties every time his father travels out of town.

I'm serious it's getting so unbearable that the other night bear had to sleep in my bed because it was giving him nightmares. I swear if this shit does not stop at 10 tonight, I won't be responsible for my actions!

After closing my journal, I walk into bear's room to see him fast asleep.

I pull my phone out and call Seth.

"Seth where are you? Do you want to come over?" I ask down the phone as music blares in the background.

"Sorry I'm at Darian's. He's having a massive Rager be round in a second with Audrey." Seth says slurring his words.

"Are you joking? you know I'm trying to study and my brother is trying to sleep while my mother works!" I hiss down the phone feeling infuriated.

"Astrid I can't hear you, come open the door!" Seth slurs as I roll my eyes and put the phone down.

Once I open the front door Audrey comes in pulling Seth along with her.

"Darian's party is so lit!" Seth exclaims, half dancing as I glare at him.

"Hey, Audrey could you watch Bear for me for a moment? I need to have a word with Darian!" I say smiling at her feeling my rage bubbling.

"Yeah, sure is it cool if I sleep over?" She asks as I nod.

I run upstairs to my room and I get changed into a pair of leggings and a crop top.

The music is so loud it's banging through my wall.

"Fuck sake!" I shout running downstairs pulling Seth with me over to Darian's.

"Darian!" I shout looking through the crowds of people.

"Darian!" I scream getting louder.

"Darian specs is here! "Some tall blonde boy says as I glare at him.

A second later Darian walks out the room doing up his jeans and I glare at him.

"Can you please turn the music down?" I ask calmly as he smirks.

"Well, let me think" he says putting his hand on his chin as I glare at him.

"No!" He snaps.

"Turn it down, my brother is asleep!" I snap as he shakes his head and I feel my blood boil.

"Not my problem!" He hisses as he walks into the garden and I follow along.

"I'm serious I will call the cops!" I say tapping his shoulder.

He turns around and moves closer to me out of fear I step back.

"Like I said specs not my fucking problem!
"He hisses as he moves closer to me. I step
back again but there's nothing to step back on
so I fall into the pool. Water splashes all over
the side and everyone erupts with laughter.

Anger pulls at me and I get out of the pool.

"You want a battle, I will give you a fucking
war! "I say getting up in Darian's face the
garden suddenly becomes completely quiet.

I walk away from him my flip flops making a
squelching noise as I move.

I get home and walk upstairs pulling out a dry
tshirt and pj shorts. I look over at my bed.
Laying in my bed are Seth and Audrey.

Ugh.

I walk downstairs and lay on the sofa drifting
deep into slumber.

I'm woken by my mother standing over me calling my name.

"What!" I hiss as I turn over on the sofa.

"Why is there a girl being sick in our bathroom and a boy snoring and dribbling on your pillow?" My mother says glaring at me as my eyes go wide and Audrey and Seth walk down the stairs.

"Mum meet my new best friends Audrey and Seth!" I say standing up off the sofa.

"It's nice to meet you." Audrey and Seth say smiling at my mother.

"Likewise, listen we are having a dinner party tonight so please dress appropriately maybe less casual and be home for 6!" Mum says as I look at her puzzled by her aberrant announcement.

"Where are we going? You never take us out to dinner?" I say confused as Seth and Audrey stand on the stairs.

"Joe from next door got back from somewhere this morning and well he invited us round for dinner." Mum says as I look at her perplexed then it hits me.

"Darian's dad!" I say as my eyes go wide.

"Yes, Astrid Darian's dad!" My mother says taking off her nursing blouse and walking into the kitchen as I follow her.

I watch as Audrey and Seth's heads peek around the doorway and they listen inquisitively.

"No mum you can't okay, please don't make me Darian is he's a Darian's a...." I mumble as my mother stands in front of me with her hand on her hip waiting impatiently.

"Well he's what?" My mother questions.

"He's a Judice mum please don't make me go!" I say begging her as Seth and Audrey snigger.

"You will attend the dinner party tonight and you will be home by six to get ready tonight do you understand?" My mother says sternly giving me the don't fuck with me look and I sigh.

"Yes, but mum" I start to say trying to plead my non-existent case.

"No buts, end of conversation Astrid!" She says as I groan and walk out the kitchen.

CHAPTER SEVEN

"This is completely unnecessary. Are we in a movie or something? We don't need to have a dinner party with our neighbours. We aren't those kinds of people who chitchat and mingle whilst having a glass of wine!" I rant whilst sliding the clothes on the sales rack at Brandy Melville as the hanger makes a cringe worthy scraping sound.

"not to mention the fact mum rang Joe and offered to host the dinner party at ours since joes going to be tired and jet-lagged, and Darian is entering through the fresh hold."

"At least she gave you some money to get some new clothes!" Audrey says looking on the bright side as Seth puts on a cute Butterfly scarf and Audrey scoffs at him.

"I saw that first!" She hisses, he glares at her.

"Well, I got it first!" He speaks.

"If I cared one microbe about cash, yeah I'd probably be a little excited but since I couldn't well I don't!" I say sighing.

"Could you at least try to be a little more optimistic? I'd freak out if the hottest guy in the whole college walked into your house tonight!" Seth says swooning as Audrey and I roll our eyes in unison.

"Ignore him, he's been in love with Darian since we were kids!" Audrey says as Seth crosses his arms whilst defensively glaring at her.

"Not true!" He says scowling as I laugh.

He rolls his eyes as I say, "It is so true!".

As Seth looks at us, he says, "Fine just a little bit!".

"He's got a different girl in his bed near on every night. I've only been here two weeks and the number of girls I see coming in and out of that house is astronomical!" I say criticising his whore-like antics.

"I don't know, I don't think he sleeps with all of them!" Seth says as Audrey sniggers.

"And now you are defending him!" She says as Seth glares at her warningly as I giggle.

" What else would they be doing playing travel scrabble!" I say as Seth finally gives in.

"Okay but maybe he only does it to seem more manly because really he's in the closet, you should ask him!" Seth says and I nod.

"That's an amazing idea Seth, I'm gonna ask him tonight in front of his father!" I say smirking.

"Astrid don't provoke him!" Audrey says sounding like my mother as I nod and put my hand on my chest.

"I won't intentionally scouts honour." I say smirking and they both chuckle.

A couple of hours later.

" Astrid they are here, come down stairs" my mother calls in a calm tone. I stand looking at myself in the mirror. God, I look so bland.

I'm wearing a grey long sleeved brandy Melville top along with some charcoal grey leggings I got from ASOS.

My chestnut dark brown hair has a slight blow-out to it after drying it with my blow-dryer.

I put my large tortoise shell black glasses on and I tuck a strand of hair behind my ear and apply some tinted cherry lip balm.

"Astrid, now!" My mother calls again, this time not sounding so calm.

My baby brother was in his high chair when I ran down the stairs to get him.

"Astrid don't be rude, come say hi to the guests!" My mother demands as I strap bear in and turn around frowning.

I look at my mother. Her hair is pulled back into a slick pony tail. Her lips are a light pink colour if I wasn't mistaken, I'd say my mother is trying to impress our guests.

"Hi you must be Astrid I'm Joe Darian's dad, it's so nice to meet you!" Joe says getting over and done with the fair-weather bullshit. I say my hello's back whilst plastering on a fake smile.

"I'm Astrid it's nice to meet you too!" I say as I look at Darian whilst talking to Joe.

"Darian" I say glaring at him almost like I'm using his name as an insult because well my mother would skin me alive if I called him a Judice to his face in front of her, that would be beneath me.

"Astrid"Darian snarls back as I glare at him and my mother leads us to the kitchen table.

"Mum may I be excused, I need to use the ladies' room" I ask as she pulls a tray of pasta bake out the cooker.

She turns around to face me and glares a warning glare.

"Of course, sweetie but don't be long." She says as she glares. I take a sip of my water and gulp.

"Right." I say as I stand up and walk out of the room.

I walk upstairs into the bathroom, I lock the door and stare at the mirror seeing the pathetic excuse of a person that's staring back at me.

I splash water over my face as I start to feel sick. I dial my father's phone number.

It is directed straight to voicemail as usual.

"Dad it's been six months since you left, I thought I'd forget about you but I haven't, I really want to, I wish I could I want to forgive you I really do, but you just hurt me you hurt mum you hurt Eli." I say playing with the case on my phone.

"It's not like you are going to hear this anyway so what's the point!" I say down the phone then click cancel answer message.

I walk out of the bathroom into my bedroom and I jump
When I see Darian sitting in my desk chair, he swivels around to face me.

"Get out of my room swine." I hiss, he smirks.

"What are these supposed to be?" Darian asks. While holding up my journals, my cheeks instantly turned red from embarrassment.

"Don't tell me you are one of those girls who writes down all her feelings because daddy ran away with his work colleague" Darian says smirking as I Glare at him.

I smack the journal out of his hand and sends it flying over the bed.

"Don't talk about my life coke head!" I snap. He gets up in my face so close I can feel his hot breath on my cheek.

"But why not, it's so fun!" He says, smirking, as I remember the plan.

"By all means go ahead and have your say on my life but be quick we got dinner to get to!" I say crossing my arms holding back on the evil laugh that I'm about to unleash.

CHAPTER EIGHT

"So, ugh, is Darian your only child?" I ask as Joe smiles.

"Yes." He says smiling as I nod and Darian glares at me.

"Quit snooping specs." He hisses and I raise my eyebrow.

Well, that was all I needed. That small remark.

"Joe have you ever thought the reason Darian has such a shitty temper is maybe because well he's not being honest with everyone!" I say smirking as I feel Darian's foot playing with mine and I smile an evil smile at him.

"Whatever do you mean?" Joe asks, as mother takes a sip of her red wine.

My mother chokes on her wine as I say grinning, "Well, I think he's in the closet so far deep, way, way in the closet."

She begins to speak but I roll my eyes and interrupt.

"Yeah, yeah I know I'm leaving." I say as I get up from the table and make my way out the living room. I start walking up the stairs and as I've just about made it to the top stair, I feel someone pull me back.

I turn and see it's Darian.

"You want to see how in the closet I am?" He says smirking pressing himself against me as he strokes my cheek.

I try to speak, but nothing comes out.

"What do you want me to do, Specs?" Darian whispers in my ear and a shiver makes its way down my spine as his hands touch my waist.

"I Ugh...I...." I try to speak but no words will come out.

"Things just got interesting." Darian says smirking as he walks away.

I follow him downstairs and a confused squeal escapes my lips as I step back.

My mother is standing at the front door kissing Darian's dad.

"WHAT THE FUCK!" Darian hisses out and my eyes go wide.

" Do you make a habit of kissing men you met two days ago mum?" I murmur as she shakes her head.

"Me and Joe have known each other since high school." Mum says as Darian rolls his eyes and for once we are in agreement on something.

"don't tell me you were high school sweethearts that could never be don't tell me you are that kind of cliche mum." I say glaring at Joe as I feel Darian's hand crawl up mine as he makes circles on my palm with his finger.

I don't have time to react to it because I'm stuck in thought.

"So, what are you two dating? When did that even begin?" I asked, feeling confused as it hits me.

"You didn't move here to get me closer to college did you? You moved here to get closer to him, to Joe, didn't you mum?" I say feeling a lump rising in my throat.

"We want to take it slow and do it right. Would you support me, Astrid?" My mother asks with hope in her eyes.

I don't say another word I don't need to; I've learnt from a young age that thoughts aren't always supposed to be spoken out loud and that you hurt a lot of people if you do so I keep my tainted and irregular thoughts in my thought journal that only my eyes can see.

I simply nod. She walks up to me and hugs me. Darian doesn't have quite the reaction I do. In fact he lets go of my hand and storms out of the house. He slams the door along the way.

"Angry! "Bear murmurs in his sweet gurgling baby voice as I let out a giggle and walk up to him. I pull a baby wipe out of the packet that's sat on the table and I take it wiping the residue of pasta off his face.

"He's always angry!" I state pulling an angry face as bear Laughs.

DEAR FUCKED UP THOUGHT VENT

Soon enough I learnt that Darian uses sex as a coping mechanism when stress comes about. It's kind of toxic and irritating at the same time because my bedroom is right next door to his house and he can see through my window and I can see through His and as much as it pains my inner soul to see what's happening the inner snoop inquisitive Harriet the spy wannabe in me always gives into that side of me and takes a peek I mean who can blame me half the time it sounds like the girl is being beaten to a pulp with all the screams and moans but i guess she likes it.

Man, sex is weird.

CHAPTER NINE

"Please bring in your assignments Monday, that's all for English class you are free to go home" Mr Webster says as the class room silently cheers.

"So, where's Audrey?" I ask Seth. Despite his small smile, I can tell that something is wrong.

"She's with her grandma in New Jersey for a month" Seth says as I can't help but laugh out loud.

"Geez Astrid morbid much!" Seth says rolling his eyes as I giggle.

"I'm sorry but you just made it seem like she died, she's only away for a month and there is such thing as FaceTime." I say shrugging unfazed.

"Why are you so calm? You're normally a ball of anxiety!" Seth exclaims as I smirk. I pull a pack of pills out of my handbag.

"Ahh, I see." He says smirking.

"Anxiety is no longer an issue my head is so fucking empty and I love it." I say smiling at him as he laughs.

"So, you're free for a party tonight?" Seth says as I huff my lips out.

"I said my head is empty not brainless, good try Seth!" I say laughing.

"Please, for me." Seth says begging.

" Oh please, beg is not a flattering colour on you!" I say sassily as he laughs.

He jumped up and down as he said, "True, now you say yes!".

"Fine, yes." I say smiling as I pull my sunglasses out of my bag and switch them with my regular ones.

Finally, it's time for a good ole fashion makeover!" Seth says with a farmer's voice and accent as I giggle.

"What'd you have in mind good sir?" I question as he smirks and raises his eyebrows.

"Just wait, baby cakes." Seth says as I laugh.

An hour later.

"Mum is it cool if Seth comes round; we are invited to a big party!" I say skipping into the kitchen, she's sat on a stall.

"Mum?" I question when she doesn't respond.

"Astrid take a seat." my mother says as I laugh.

"Sorry mum this is going to have to wait, I got party stuff to plan." I say running upstairs.

Ten minutes later.

"Okay so I brought a couple of outfits for you. We have the simple but cute short black dress." Seth says smiling as I shake my head.

"No, I'm not heading to a funeral," I reply, rolling my eyes.

"Okay so I have this cute red crop top and black leather shorts." Seth says as I nod.

As I laughed, Seth asked, "Really you like?" smiling optimistic

"Yeah, no" I say as he glares at me.

"Finally last but not least a cute black denim skirt and a plain grey long sleeved crop top from Brandy Melville!" Seth says as I smile widely.

"Perfect!" I say smiling a sweet smile and he rolls his eyes.

"Fine, take a shower, get changed then I will do your hair and makeup!" Seth instructs as I nod and hold my hand up to my head to salute him.

After showering and letting Seth do my makeup and hair, I am finally ready.

I run downstairs along with Seth.

"Bye mum." I say walking out the front door with Seth.

We get into Seth's old Vauxhall Astra and my phone starts to ring. It's Eli. I roll my eyes and put the phone down.

"Who was that?" Seth asks as I push my full blow-out 70s style hair out my face.

"Just my brother, he's probably ringing to talk about what girl he's sleeping with this week." I say laughing.

"I didn't know you had another brother." Seth says looking at me intrigued as I nod.

"Yep, I do unfortunately!" I say laughing.

"Is he single or bi or gay, oh my god please say he is gay!" Seth says getting excited as I roll my eyes.

"He's straight but he is definitely not your type!" I state matter of factly.

"You don't know, he could be!" Seth says winking at me, I shriek.

"Okay, okay enough talking about you wanting to hook up with Eli. "I say as he laughs and parks the car outside the house we are partying at.

"Okay so what did we practice?" Seth says looking at me as I smile feeling proud that I learned his patronising instructions for how to not embarrass him at a party.

I say, "For one, don't beg to go home!".

"Well done," He says proudly.

"Two, don't fall over like the first day at college." I say rolling my eyes as he claps his hands.

"Okay next." He says impatiently.

"Three, don't fight with Darian if we see him because he's the love of your life and you won't choose between your best friend and soulmate." I say smirking knowing I'd fight with Darian anytime regardless of Seth or not.

"Good I like the part you added at the end, extra points for that!" He says smiling.

"Okay and lastly if you throw up and pass out don't ditch you!" I say as he nods.

"Thats a smart girl." Seth says patting my head as I glare at him.

"Don't push it!" I say as he steps out of his white, beat-up car and he smirks.

"Oh, oh I forgot to say a rule!" Seth says as I roll my eyes and we stop outside the door.

"Okay let's move on then." I say tapping my feet impatiently.

He leans forward and pulls my hair tie from my hair.

"Hey!" I say trying to get it back as he wiggles his finger in front of my face.

"Nope, not today Astrid it's party time let your hair down, literally!" He says as I roll my eyes and knock on the front door.

We walk into the house and it's much larger than I expected with silver walls covering each angle of the house. It's pretty. The first thing I noticed was the white diamond chandelier which indicates that the house is owned by very rich people. Music's blaring and I recognise this song and bop my head a few times as Seth moves his hands left and right dancing into the kitchen.

"Run baby run forever we'll be, you and me."
Me and Seth scream at each other jumping up
and down excitedly.

Check Yes Juliet keeps playing and I can't
help but feel comfortable with my
surroundings.

"Jones thanks for inviting us, man!" Seth says
pulling me by the hand over to the kitchen to
meet his friend.

He's very tall with curly light brown hair and
light brown eyes.

"Yeah, no problem, bro who's this?" He
questions shifting his gaze from Seth to me.

"Astrid, nice to meet you" I shout over the
music and he moves close to me and takes my
hand shaking it sloppily in a drunken manner.

I look past him at Seth motioning for me to grow some balls and ask him for a drink.

"Umm Jones could you I Ugh do you think?" I say stuttering as Seth moves closer to me and puts his foot on top of mine. I Yelp a bit.

"Yeah?" Jones shouts over the music holding onto my shoulder like I'm one of the bros.

"Do you maybe want to get a drink?" I say as he nods.

"Yeah totally!" He says totally wasted.

CHAPTER TEN

Half an hour passes and me and Seth are both drunk dancing with each other as a Paramore song plays.

My phone starts to ring. It's been ringing all night. It's probably my mother asking me to babysit but for one night I want to be a teenager.

I'm dancing and jumping up and down with Seth when Darian storms in through the front door. In a quick attempt to remain unseen by him I make a b line for the kitchen.

It doesn't work because I feel someone tapping my shoulder.

"Hi Darian I didn't see you there." I say turning around on my heels to face him trying to play it cool.

"You need to come with me." He hisses as I roll my eyes.

"You can beg as much as you want but dude it isn't going to change my mind, I won't screw you on the weekends." I mutter drunkenly as Seth high-fives me.

"Astrid stop fucking around, your mum sent me to get you, something has happened." Darian says looking at me nervously.

"What now she wants me to babysit again, can't I have fun for one night?" I say walking past him grabbing a red Solo cup of whatever alcohol is available at arm's reach.

"Astrid please it's your dad." Darian says as I stop.

"W..... what?" I question turning around feeling my blood boil at the sound of the word dad.

Growing up my father was never the affectionate type. It took 16 years for him to finally say he loved me back.

But when my father left, he explained to me and Eli how much he loved Susan. He told us with such eager anticipation. He said it like he was telling us we were going to get a puppy for Christmas or that Santa Claus is real. Being my parents' only children had both advantages and disadvantages. For example, Eli was my father's favorite, and I was my mother's.

When my father left, things changed things got more complicated, things I never worried about before suddenly became increasingly anxiety-inducing. The anxiety got so overwhelming that I was put on this new medication to make me feel nothing except the medication said nothing about the side-effects of drinking with it.

"Darian, I don't feel to.........." I start to say as I see a few white dots in front of my eyes and everything becomes blurry and dark.

I feel myself being carried.

"Oh, Batman you are so strong." I mumble falling back into his chest.

I wake up a brief while later in a bed.

I sit up and my head starts to pound like there's a tiny man in there banging a hammer onto my skull.

I look down at the duvet that's messily draped over me, the duvets dark brown. I shrug and lay back down knowing I'm in Seth's room.

"Good, you're awake." Someone says walking into the bedroom and shutting the door.

"Oh my god." I mumble knowing the face behind the voice.

I don't look up or even attempt to get up. I simply close my eyes and open them again, hoping this is some crazy night terror.

Nope.

He walks over to the bed with a bottle of water in his hand and a packet of paracetamol.

"Are those for me?" I question sitting up and pulling the duvet cover up a notch just in case I was no longer wearing my skirt.

"Yep." He says as I take them off him and pop the lid off the water bottle.

After swallowing the pills, I look at Darian and I notice his jaw tense.

"Why am I here, where's Seth?" I find myself becoming increasingly confused.

"You got wasted I told you that your father had died you passed out, your friend left with some guy and I was stuck with you calling me Batman half the night." Darian says as I laugh a bit then stop dead still.

"Did you say my father?" I ask as he nods and I scramble to my feet.

I'm up next to him in a matter of seconds.

"You are full of shit my brother would've told me, my mum." I snap as he gets closer to me and leans down.

"They did, check your phone specs." He says as I shake my head.

"You're a liar, fuck you!" I hissed walking away from him making my way to his bedroom door.

He grabs my arm before I even have a chance to say anything and he pulls me back to him.

"He's dead Astrid, except it and move on!" Darian says with a frigid glare.

"You sick asshole, don't say that!" I snap getting ready to leave once again.

He remains quiet but hands me my phone.

I have thirty miss calls from Eli and twenty-two from mum seven from Susan and three from Seth.

I look at a text from my mum.

Astrid, come home right now, something terrible has happened.

No.

No.

No.

I look at the smug look on Darian's face then down at the stupid band t shirt I'm wearing.

"I hate you!" I shout running up to him as he stays still with his arms crossed completely unfazed. He unfolded his arms after I hit him.

I continue to hit his chest crying and screaming.

"I hate you, I hate you, I hate you, I hate you." I shriek as he grabs me by the arms and holds me still.

"Astrid we both know that's not true." He says as tears pour down my cheeks and I pull my arm away from him wiping my eyes.

"Why did you bring me here? I could've gone home." I say quietly not looking at him.

"No, you couldn't your mums with my dad and you were puking everywhere. I don't think your mother would be okay seeing you like that." He says as I look at him.

"Where's my bag, my clothes, I need to leave" I say looking at myself in his mirror as I see the mascara in crusty blobs mixed with tears on my cheeks.

"Your bag and your clothes are on the table. I washed the clothes last night." He says as I nod.

"I need to get home." I say looking at him as he nods.

I walk out of the bedroom and down the stairs, I grab my bag and keys off the table and out of the house.

I walk next door and attempt to unlock my front door with shaky hands. It's difficult to get the key into the lock but I finally unlock it.

There's no noise in the house it's completely silent.

I open the door and walk inside.

I walk up to the countertop.

Astrid, we drove to the hospital with your brother Joes and took Bear to school. Don't do anything stupid, I love you.

Don't do anything stupid.

I read the last part of the note out loud to myself because every fibre of my body is telling me to do something stupid.

I ran upstairs to my bedroom and looked at myself in the large Victorian mirror I'd gotten at an old boot sale and mum painted it white for me.

Mascara's smudged down my cheeks my chestnut brown hairs knotted and tangled. I scream in anger hating every inch of the reflection I see.

I stare down at Darian's stupid T-shirt and I pull it off me with rage, throwing it onto the floor. How can someone say such a thing "except it and move on"? God, I hate him.

Is that how little people mean to him?

Is that how little I mean to him?

CHAPTER ELEVEN

DEAR FUCKED UP THOUGHT VENT

I FUCKED UP

My father got into a fight at the bar and he got punched in the nose and then punched again then punched again.

Punched until he was no longer conscious.

He was then taken to the Hospital where Eli and mum got to say goodbye to him. He passed away at around 2am when I was passed out drunk in Darian's bed.

The doctors and nurses said he was punched in the nose so hard his nose bone slipped out of place and punctured his brain.

Regardless, aside from crying in front of Darian, that was the only time I wept. My mother embraced me and she decided that was the right time for me to cry. I never shed a tear since I left Darian's house that day, and it's been the same ever since.

"Astrid come down we are leaving." mum calls as I put my pen down and shut my journal.

"Ready?" Mum asks as my brother ignores my presence.

"Yes," I say quietly as I look down at my black shiny shoes.

Come on Astrid cry at the funeral that's what normal people do. Come on be normal.

We pull up outside the church. It's funny my father's funeral is in a church since he cheated on his wife and lied to our faces for months. I was pretty sure lying was a sin but maybe I was wrong.

I pick Bear up in my arms and pull the bottom of my black dress down and walk in.

We sit through the part where the priest says that my father was an honourable man. He was an honest man and a loving husband. All eyes in the church are on me as I snigger.

"I'm sorry for our loss, Astrid" Susan says coming up to me as I glare at her and plaster a fake smile on my face.

"Thank you, I'm sorry for my mother's loss as-well." I say turning on my heels and walking away from her.

God, please make me cry now. It would be the most appropriate time to cry.

Nope not a single tear.

"Eli, Astrid please come and say some kind words about your father." The priest says as Eli gets up and I follow him once we are on the podium. I try to hide behind me but it's no use because every time I step behind him, he moves away from me bringing more attention to us.

Once Eli has said his kind words it's my turn. I swallow down the dry lump in my throat and cough.

He Ugh he was my dad." I say, trying to find some kind words to say.

I should do what I always do, and dwell on my past father, who I knew before the cheating, lying, and abandoning.

But not this time.

"My dad wasn't a lovable man it took me years to tell him I loved him it took him even longer to say he loved me, I don't ever remember him telling me his feelings, he wasn't a feelings kind of dad, he was a do it kind of dad fixer upper, you broke your tooth he'll book you in at the dentist, you need a wardrobe built he'll build it for you, well not now he won't but you get what I mean he wasn't affectionate he wasn't really in touch with his feelings I guess I am like my father in that way because I can't fucking cry and I know why because I can't find a small part of me to feel guilt or sorry for a man who left his family then left this earth." I say as everyone gasps.

"Yeah, I get it aunt Judie and uncle Jake I managed to screw up saying one pleasant thing about my father, I'm sorry." I say looking into the crowd as the distant relatives and family friends look at me in shock, disgust and anguish.

"It's kind of laughable when you think about it. No, not an honest man. He cheated on his wife of twenty-one years, caring also nope." I say as Eli prys the mic out of my hand.

"That's enough Astrid!" He hisses as I glare at him.

"Why because daddy's favourite says so, well fuck you, fuck you all for lying and speaking kind words. He was a terrible person. You don't always have to honour the dead. Just because they are dead doesn't make them any less horrible!" I say as my mother cries on and on, I look at her in the corner.

I stop.

"I, I Ugh I, I am sorry." I say mumbling as I get down from the podium and make my way out of the church.

I sit on the short wall outside the church holding my journal in my hands. I take my pen out and start to write.

DEAR FUCKED UP THOUGHT VENT

I told you I had unorthodox thoughts.

Well for once my unorthodox thoughts pulled themselves off the pages and rolled off my tongue. I'm pretty sure that my mother is planning to disown me, I'm a disappointment.

Fuck.

My dad's probably in hell because there's no way he made it to the pearly gates in sky with all the shit, he did and he's probably looking up and thinking how much he hates me.

I'd hate me, I do hate me.

Fuck.

I screw up all the time.

The first time my father cheated on my mother was when I was seven. He took me to the local pub I think it was called the moonbeam inn. I think her name was Ellen. She was a nasty woman.

She was mean and scary. She'd give me dirty looks and call me fat when my father wasn't looking.

I refused to make eye contact the whole time I was at the bar with my father. I simply sat there calmly hunched over in the uncomfortable wooden seat eating a half pack of out-of-date cheese and onion crisps from the back of the store unit that the nasty woman had given me because she wasn't gracious enough to give me the brand-new ones but it was free food and I loved food.

Anyway, she and my father had to discuss something in the restroom. By discuss, I mean fuck. Back then I didn't know that it was so wrong and I thought they were just talking.

So, I told my mother.

Not intentionally but because I was excited and proud that my father actually bothered with me and well after that it would be a cycle my father would cheat and my mother would sometimes find out when she did, she'd sometimes cry sometimes slap his cheek. I'd secretly enjoy the slap because it was enjoyable to watch him getting his comeuppance even if it was minuscule.

And then they'd make up until the next time.

It stopped at Susan because he fell for her and fled. As a family, we were broken and dysfunctional but we were making it work. We always made it work with or without him.

Until he died.

He had to fuck everything up, even from the grave.

CHAPTER TWELVE

I look up from my journal and close it seeing Darian standing next to me.

"Fuck you,oh and fuck you all?" Darian replies, quoting what I said as I put my hands on my head. I sigh.

In hope of getting his interpretation from his perspective, I ask: "Was it that disastrous from your viewpoint?".

He nods.

Fuck.

Darian says as I roll my eyes and push my glasses up my nose to stop them from falling down: "Yeah, I mean definitely, but in all respects it was pretty entertaining. You should join drama club." I roll my eyes and push my glasses up my nose.

"At least I gave you entertainment dickface!" I say crossing my arms as he chuckles.

"Very ladylike." He says and I roll my eyes.

"Hey, a small tip on the crying thing." He says turning to me before he walks away.

"Yeah?" I question. At this point I'll take advice from anyone even if it is my sworn enemy.

"No crying don't, that dick doesn't deserve your tears." He says as I nod and smile a small smile he turns away and walks off.

As I giggle, Eli snaps, "What the heck was that Astrid, daddy's favorite?".

"You got to admit it was a wee bit funny?" I replied smugly.

"You are so fucked in the head you know that, your dad just died and you are laughing and acting like nothing happened!" He says bitterly as I glare at him.

"Yep, I'm fucked in the head, why don't you tell me something I don't know? "Oh and by the way dad cheated on mum before Susan with April the head administrator for the college you are at so basically you are there on hand outs just like me pal sucks doesn't it knowing you got something from cheating, lies and deception." I say smugly as he glares at me.

"You aren't morally higher or better than me Eli just because you saw a side to dad that I didn't, doesn't mean I'm below you." I say honestly as he shakes his head.

He gets up in my face taking his pointer finger and shoving it into the side of my temple.

"No but this fucked up thing makes you morally below me because I know the things you think aren't normal, you are so fucked up!" He shouts as I shut my eyes and jump down from the ledge that I'm sitting on.

"Too far Eli." I mumble out as I walk away.

I walk home in the rain and feel no tears in my eyes.

I get outside and look over at Darian's house.

I take my chance and knock on the front door.

But no one answers.

"Darian?" I call again, but no answer.

Without thinking I open the door and walk in.

He's not in the front room.

He's not in the kitchen.

I walk upstairs and hear no noise.

"Darian?" I say storming into his room my eyes go wide when I see his hand stroking up and down on himself as he throws his head back in pleasure.

"Astrid!" He cries in panic as he releases.

"Oh my, fuck!" I cry so hard for the first time in two weeks tears escape my eyes.

I slam his bedroom door and run down the stairs falling on the last two steps. I fall on my ass and my cheeks go bright red. I don't hesitate to get up because I'm too mortified to stay.

I pace up and down on our front lawn.

I look up at the window to see him looking down at me smirking.

Oh my god.

I ran into my house; I saw my mother sitting on the sofa with Bear.

"Where's Eli?" I asked, trying to distract myself from whatever it was that I just witnessed.

"He's gone back to college what you did Astrid it was........" she starts to say as I stop her.

"Yeah, mum I get it. I was stupid and thoughtless. I will send everyone an apology message and say I'm in mourning." I say as she shakes her head.

"Astrid I was about to say how it was brave of you, you hide your feelings in those silly old journals of yours since you were seven and you've been having to deal with your father's lies for years. I'm proud of you and I just wish I was as honest as you were! "My mother says as I nod.

"Mum you are brave you are strong you swallowed your feelings for years and kept our house whole for the sake of us you put your feelings last." I say as she smiles and pats the empty seat to the left of her. I smile and walk over sitting down.

She hugs me tightly.

"It's over Astrid we can be a normal family now." She says as I shake my head.

"How about we can just be a family, Normal's overrated anyway." I say as she laughs.

"Sounds good to me." She says smiling.

CHAPTER THIRTEEN

DARIAN'S POV

It's been a month since her father's funeral and no one's noticed a thing but I did, I've noticed.

She's changed, she's thinner, she has heavy bags under her eyes. She puts her EarPods in during class and when I have loud parties when my dad's out of town she doesn't fuss.

She's been shutting her bedroom curtains every day, when I knock her over after class like I used to she doesn't flinch and she doesn't react. It's like a switch has flipped off in her brain and she's turned off any emotions.

I saw her today and told her my father and I are coming over for dinner tomorrow and she just shrugged it off and walked away.

I don't know what's going on and I can't read her but the real question is, why in the world do I want to?

Why do I care?

A day later.

ASTRID'S POV

I wake up after a restless night.

Things don't feel the same. I feel guilty I haven't spoken to Eli and I can't seem to get my father out of my mind.

I pull myself out of bed and run a bath since it's Saturday and I have no classes and I have nothing to do till tonight's dinner party.

I sit in my moderately hot bath with my knees to my face feeling depressed.

I screw up.

It's simple.

Your father just died even if he never cared about you or he was a terrible person. Therefore, you don't try and upset everyone he loved to get some kind of sick revenge.

And what if he hates me?

What if?

Why do I never stop thinking even late at night? My mind just never shuts up.

"I can do things no human can do; I can doubt myself then I'll doubt you that's nothing new."

"Watch me as I go and separate the ones that I am made to love and hate slowly counting down my body weight I'm tired."

I sing the song quietly to myself feeling numbness overtake me.

There's a knock on the bathroom door.

"Who is it?" I call out pulling my head away from my knees.

"It's mum, I need you to watch Bear whilst I go out to get something for the dinner party tonight." Mum says as I sigh.

"Yes mum, I will be out in a second" I say quietly as I hear footsteps.

I sit and contemplate, that's something I've always been skilled at since childhood.
Just thinking.

When will I stop thinking?

I shut my eyes and shoved my head deep under the water.

My mother calls me, and I pull my head up out of the water, breathing heavy.

"Just getting out the bath now I will come down in a second!" I call out to my mother.

Sighing I pull the plug out and stand up getting out of the bath.

I wrap my towel around my body and I walk to my bedroom.

I put on an old vintage brown sweatshirt and a pair of black leggings.

"Listen if Darian and Joe show up early, entertain them whilst I get the food." Mum says as I nod.

"Okay." I mumble.

An hour later.

"Hello Astrid, wake up!" Someone calls as I turn around and cuddle with bear on his bed.

"Astrid!" I hear someone whisper again but this time louder.

I sit up in the bed to see Darian over me.

"What?" I ask rubbing my eyes to remove any eye boogers.

"My dad is heading to pick your mum up from the store - she's having car trouble!" he says as I nod and pull the duvet over us.

"Aren't you getting up?" He questions as I shake my head.

"What's the point in that?" I question as I look down at his shoes then up at him I see disappointment in his eyes.

"I'm having a party tomorrow when dad is not around, are you intending to narc on me?" He says smirking as I shake my head.

"No, what's the point in that as well?" I say as I turn around and shut my eyes.

A second later I feel the bed sink a bit.

"What are you doing?" I ask opening my eyes peaking up to see Darian sitting on the side of the bed.

"What's going on with you, Astrid?" He questions as I look at him.

"Like you care!" I huff.

"That's the issue, I do." He says as I look at him.

"Well, I'm fine thanks for the inquiry." I say quietly as I get up from the bed quietly walking out of bear's bedroom leaving him to finish his nap.

"I will make things easier on you if that's what you need." Darian says following after me as I scoff.

"Don't bother doing me any favours." I say huffing walking down the stairs into the kitchen.

"Please tell me how I can help you." He asks as I turn to him.

"Darian, why are you here?" I say turning round to face him.

"You haven't been the same." He says quietly looking at me like a scared little boy.

"OK." I say as I turn around and pull out the knives and forks from the drawer, setting them up on the table.

"You can cry Astrid; you don't always have to be strong even if the tears aren't for him." He says walking up to me.

"I can't cry, I want to but I can't because the mood meds I'm on make my tears null and void." I say looking down at the floor.

"Why are you being kind to me?" I question looking up at him as he chuckles lowly.

"Shhh you're about to jinx it." Darian says as I smirk a little.

CHAPTER FOURTEEN

"So, are you two still dating?" I question looking at my mother as she shakes her head.

"No, it would be disrespectful to just disregard any feelings that I had for you father." My mother says as my heart grows cold by the second.

I feel Darian's hand on my thigh and I look up at him.

'Yes, mom, I'm glad you value your values.' I murmur as she smiles back at me.

"So, guys this dinner has been so enjoyable, but boy oh boy am I tired "I mumble out as they all look at me including bear who begins to laugh at me as I stick my tongue out.

"Astrid we've just sat down; you will have to excuse my daughters she's......" my mum says stopping and thinking of a word.

"In mourning?" I question as she nods and points her fork at me.

"That, she's in mourning." Mum says putting down her fork and picking up her red wine as Joe nods.

"Well, it was nice that you joined us, Astrid!" Joe says smiling and I nod.

"Could I be excused too?" Darian asks as His dad nods.

I'm half way walking up the stairs when Darian pulls my hand back.

"What?" I murmur turning around and looking at him.

"I need to talk to you" he says as he walks ahead of me.

"What do you want to talk about Darian?" I question.

"I can't get Erin off my fucking back!" Darian says as he looks at me expecting me to know what his talking about.

"And, I'm supposed to care why?" I mumble sitting down on my bed.

"I figured maybe we could do something to help each other out!" Darian says as I scoff.

"And what in the world could you do for me?" I asked with a hint of sarcasm in my voice.

"I see how poorly you get treated in college." Darian says as I scoff.

"Yeah, I really wonder why!" I mumble as he smirks.

"What if you could be my distraction? Then I will get you popular!" Darian says and I laugh.

"And what makes you think I have one microbe of care about popularity?" I ask, crossing my arms for the second time.

"I know you don't but I do however see how you look at Jones." Darian says and my cheeks flush.

"So?" I say glaring at him.

"He will be into you within the next two months with the help of me that is! "He says and I roll my eyes.

"And what do I have to do for you?" I question as a wide grin spreads across his face.

"You have to pretend to be my girlfriend." He states and my eyes grow wide.

"Yeah, that's not going to happen!" I say glaring at him.

"Just think about it." He says and begins to walk out of my bedroom. I call him back.

"Yeah? "He says turning to look at me.

"I thought about it!" I say smiling.

"And?" He asks.

"Still no!" I say sticking my middle finger up.

"Fine, but you will change your mind." He says walking down the stairs as I stand at the top of the landing.

"I doubt it." I shout down to him as he smirks.

The rest of the week was spent avoiding everyone. Darin would write me notes asking if I'd thought about the plan to which I would toss them in the bin.

To also prove his point Darian pushed me over in the canteen and Jones laughed his head off without a word. Darian smugly winked at me and walked off.

I'm about to walk home when I see Darian standing by his car talking to some blonde preppy cheer girl. I roll my eyes and storm over to him.

"We need to talk," I say, and he nods without saying a word.

"Right, meet me in a few," I opined.

Without another word I walk off and make my way home shoving my headphones in.

I get home and it is empty. The sweet, sweet sound of peace and quiet.

"What the hell!" I murmur hearing the loud sound of thudding on the front door.

I look through the peep hole and see it's Darian.

"Do you have to bang like that?" I snapped, letting him in.

Grinning boyishly, he said, "I wanted too!".

"Okay well you scared me." I say walking into the kitchen with Darian falling not far behind me.

"Sorry." He says and I turn to him.

"Do you want a drink? I got an orange juice box?" I asked, pulling the juice box out of the fridge.

"Sure." He says as I throw him it and he instantly catches it.

"Show off." I mumble.

"So, what do you want to talk to me about specs?" Darian says smirking.

I ask, "How long would the whole favor thing have to last?".

"After February, you are free then." He says as I look at him confused.

"Erin will want me to be with her for Valentine's Day. If I'm fake dating you she won't be able to be with me." He says and I nod.

"I won't have to sleep with you?" I question and he shakes his head.

"Not even if you beg me." He says winking and I make a puke face.

"Not likely." I speak.

"Then we won't have a problem." He states and I nod.

"So, what I suggest is you write me a list of do's and don'ts and I write you one you come over tomorrow to discuss business, do we have a deal?" Darian asks raising his eyebrow.

"Shoot I got to pick bear up, deal!" I murmur grabbing my handbag flinging it on my back and rushing out the front door, waiting for Darian to follow.

"Today junior!" I mumble and he rolls his eyes and moves slower.

CHAPTER FIFTEEN

"So, what you two are talking about now, I thought you hated each other, weird that you are hanging out" Seth says glaring at me over FaceTime as I laugh and the doorbell starts to ring.

Ironically, I do hate him.

Well kind of.

"I know it's kind of strange but we have to try to get on we are neighbours for goodness' sake! "I say as Seth laughs at me along with Aubrey on FaceTime.

"Yeah, I don't know, I'd say you have a crush on him" Aubrey says smirking whilst painting her nails.

"Oh my god Aubrey, you got me all figured out am I that transparent" I say sarcastically rolling my eyes.

Aubrey says, "You are more transparent than this clear nail polish named clear dream, which has the literal meaning of transparent dream" as Seth laughs hysterically.

"Anyway, I must cut this invigorating brief meeting short because Darian's here and I've kept him waiting five minutes already"

"Ooo go see him baby girl go get that capital D" Aubrey chants and I roll my eyes and start to laugh.

"Yeah, yeah whatever, see you Monday Seth text in the group chat bye" I say putting the phone down.

I walk downstairs and open the front door.

"What took you so long? I've been waiting ten minutes" Darian says glaring at me as I roll my eyes.

I could've sworn it was five minutes, oh well.

"Are you coming in or what?" I question as he scowls at me.

"No let me just stand out here for ten more minutes" he snaps as I roll my eyes and he follows me in doors.

"Have you written down your rules?" I ask and he nods.

"Okay, you state yours I say yes or no then I tell you mine." He says and I nod.

"Fine my rules no sex, no sleeping with other girls I couldn't deal with that humiliation, no flirting with other girls, you can't ask about my personal life and I won't pine to know yours; you have to pick Bear up with me from school because he likes you, and my mother can't know about this." I say and he nods.

"Okay fairs, my turn." He says grinning as my stomach churns and I start to wonder if it was a sound idea after.

"You have to make it seem like we've slept together when you talk to my mates, couldn't have them moving in on the chick slayers girl." He says smirking holding onto my arm gently as I internally cringe and get the ick.

"The fact that you call yourself the chick slayer nauseates me." I replied, slipping out of his grip.

"You have to do stuff to make Erin jealous." He says as I stop him.

"Like what?" I ask sounding completely clueless as he palms his hands.

"You know flirting like cheek kisses and stuff." He says as I nod.

"Oh, and you have to come to parties with me, we can only hate each other when we are one hundred percent sure we are alone, oh and no catching feelings I know how clingy girls can get." He says as I roll my eyes.

"We have to spend New Year's together." He says as I shake my head.

"No I always spend New Year's alone, I hate it." I say crossing my arms.

"What sort of Scrooge hates New Year's?" He says glaring at me.

"Scrooge hated Christmas dumbass, and I just don't like fireworks. They are loud and they make me anxious. They aren't safe for the environment and the only pretty thing about them is they are pretty flipping annoying!" I say as he laughs.

"Okay so we won't watch the fireworks we will do something else." He says and I roll my eyes.

"I don't get why you want to spend New Year's with me" I say and he chuckles.

"It's all part of the plan Astrid and you already shook on it, can't go back now." He says and I roll my eyes.

"Fine then you have to put the Christmas tree up with me and bear, we are a couple days late and bears upset mums working overtime so I can ...." I try to explain and he stops me.

"I'm in." He says grinning.

Well, I have to pick up Bear if you would like to take me" I say, and he shakes his head.

"Sorry, specs deal doesn't start till Monday." He says and I glare at him.

"Of course it doesn't, dick." I murmur.

CHAPTER SIXTEEN

DEAR FUCKED UP THOUGHT VENT

It's Monday morning, today's the day I have been dreading. Today, I have to walk into college with Darian and I have to act like we are in love. This should be interesting.

I only have a couple days left at college till Christmas break. I'm nervous I mean I've never had a boyfriend even if it's a fake one.

Anyway, got to run, that's my ride.

"Come on bear let's go!" I say picking up my brother off his play mat.

The horn on Darian's car sounds loudly and I roll my eyes. This is going to be a long day.

"Taxi, taxi." Bear chants excitedly.

"Yeah, I wish it was a taxi." I mumble as bear giggles.

"Come on what's the wait!" Darian shouts as I shove my middle finger up.

This whole couple thing, it's not going to work.

"Can you quit hurrying me? I got to get his seat belt on, god knows I have to with how you drive!" I snap as he glares at me.

"Well maybe if you'd quit screwing around with all your girly makeup stuff." He says chuckling as I smirk.

"Well shit, you got me all figured out." I hiss knowing full well the only make up I have on today is lip balm and concealer.

"How is this going to work assface?" I ask, looking at Darian as I get in next to him and Bear giggles.

He says, as I glare at him and he smirks, "If you would quit arguing with me all the time, this simple deal would work just perfectly, so then you can get back to whatever boring shit you do in your life.".

"Whatever." I hissed, crossing my arms.

After dropping Bear off at school, Darian drives us to the college.

"Ready?" He says as I sigh but nod.

He gets out the car first walking over to my side, he opens the door and I look at him confused.

Once I get out of the car, he grabs hold of my hand.

"Oh, what a gentleman!" I say fake swooning as he rolls his eyes.

"Oh my god!" A tall blonde-haired girl says as we walk past her.

"Darian, everyone's staring at us." I murmur as he huffs.

"Get real Astrid, you love this, all the attention!" He says smirking at me as I internally cringe.

"God Darian, you know me so well!" I say stroking his chest as everyone stares.

"Tone it down!" He hisses.

"Right, sorry!" I murmur.

"Oh, my fucking god!" Seth says as I feel my cheeks heat up red.

"Hey Seth, you've met Darian, right?" I say as he holds onto my hand.

"I've been to a couple of his parties" Seth says narrowing his eyes at Darian.

"That's great!" I say making small talk or attempting to.

"So, you two are a couple, huh?" Seth says sounding not very convinced.

"Yep, we're in love!" I say smiling a false smile as Darian treads on my foot and a Yelp escapes my lips.

"I got class, Astrid, are you coming?" Seth says as I nod.

"Yes, just a moment, I'll catch up." I say smiling as a smirk quivers on Darian's lips.

He pulls me into a free class room.

"Would you loosen up? You aren't convincing anybody!" Darian snaps glaring at me as I roll my eyes.

"Oh please, it doesn't look like you're doing any better treading on my foot like that, it hurt you know!" I hiss out.

"I was doing way better than you!" He snaps and I chuckle.

"I bet you ain't got one romantic bone in that stupid body of yours!" I say smugly.

"Umm, you think huh?" He questions getting closer to me as I feel his eyes scroll down my body examining the thrift shop green and black stripped sweater I'm wearing along with my black skinny jeans. I suddenly became very self-conscious.

"I wouldn't say it if I didn't think it. ugh you are so infuriating!" I snap as he gets closer to me. I immediately close my mouth, unable to utter another word.

He leans down and kisses the exposed skin on my neck lightly as a gasp escapes my lips. His hand grazes the hem of my jeans as he rubs my hip bone with his fingers. He leans up with a Curt grin and holds his hands behind his back that a step back.

"See I can be romantic." He says as I nod but don't answer.

I huff out as he asks, "We got a party tonight. Luca invited us. Do you think you can handle it?".

"Oh please of course I can handle it!" I say crossing my arms knowing I will ring him tonight and pretend to be ill.

"Well done specs!" He says and with that walks off.

The second he leaves the classroom, Seth walks in with a small glare on his face.

"I thought you, I mean we had class!" I say still a tiny bit in shock over such a small sign of affection from Darian a moment ago.

"You two slip out for a quickie huh?" Seth says narrowing his eyes at me.

Oops I completely forgot about Seth's lifelong crush on Darian.

"Seth please don't hate me!" I say getting ready to explain myself with a bunch of idle excuses that I'll have to make up on the spot, but he interrupts.

"You know he's been my one true love since I was like six!" Seth says as I nod and bite my bottom lip, clutching the secret at the top of my tongue.

"Did I tell you about the time in high school the football team beat me up for being gay and Darian saved me and ended up getting beat up with me?" Seth says as I feel my heart warm a bit.

"He did?" I question as Seth nods but continues to scowl at me.

"Oh, please you've liked him for five minutes I've loved him for an eternity!" Seth admits being over dramatic.

"I'm faking it!" I murmur trying to shut him up as he continues to ramble on about our friendship.

"You what?" Seth says as I look at him.

"I am faking the relationship, it's not real!" I say and a loud gasp escapes his lips.

"How could you play the love of my life like that Astrid?" Seth asks as I roll my eyes.

"Oh, please Seth read between the lines, we are both faking it and I just broke rule one by telling you!" I snap as he smirks.

"I'm so glad you are my best friend but also why did he pick you and not me I mean look at me!" He says as I roll my eyes as he does a small twirl ending in jazz hands.

"I don't know Seth he must be completely clueless!" I say as we laugh and start to walk to class.

"So, are you planning to come to Luca's big party tonight, with me?" Seth asks as I shake my head.

"As if, do I look like the party type?" I ask as he smirks.

"These days you have been surprising me more and more!" He says as I lightly tap him on the arm and he chuckles.

CHAPTER SEVENTEEN

"Ready? "I inquired looking at my mother for her support as I lay still on the sofa with my duvet over me and a warm flannel on my head.

"Yeah" she says as I pull the flannel off my head and stuff it down the sofa cushion. She turns to open the front door and I see Darian standing waiting for me.

"Ready?" Darian questions looking at me lying on the sofa as i cough.

Cough, groan, cough, groan.

"I'm just(cough) feeling so ill." I murmur as he chuckles.

"That's ace, nice try now go get ready!" He snaps as I pull the duvet off me and stand up in a huff. I glare at him.

"But I'm burning up!" I declare as he leans over me and pulls the flannel from behind the cushion.

"Fine, asshole!" I say mumbling that last part.

Half an hour later

I'm sat in the mirror applying a swipe of blusher to the apples of my cheeks when Darian walks into my room casually.

"Well come in why don't you!" I hissed, turning back to glare at him.

"You look." He starts to say and stutters.

"I look?" I question narrowing my eyes at him knowing it's going to be some kind of insult.

Trying not to offend me, he says, "Like a girl, you look like i mean you understand what I mean!" I nod slightly in agreement.

I look back at myself in the mirror showing my long sleeve black cropped jumper along with my black denim skirt.

"Well, I figured since I'm signing up for the whole college experience I might as well play out this deal properly! "I say as he nods in agreement.

"That's great Astrid." Darian says smirking.

"What?" I question narrowing my eyes at him again.

"Nothing you just look different. "He says as I smile a bit and feel my cheeks tint.

"Okay are you planning to chat me to death or take me to this party of yours?" I snort cockily as he grins.

"Option two." He says grinning.

"Smart choice." I murmur as I make my way down the stairs with him following behind.

"Oh, sweetie you look lovely!" My mother says putting her hands together.

This time I actually made an effort so it's not the most unbelievable compliment.

"Thanks mum." I mumble letting a smile spread across my cheeks.

"She will be back in time to watch bear at ten." Darian says as mum nods.

"Thank you, Darian, that's very responsible of you!" My mother says as I roll my eyes, you wouldn't think I'm nearly twenty.

"Are you okay?" Darian asks as I sit in the passenger seat of his car.

"Yes." of course I'm okay, I'm distracted.

"Don't worry everyone will love you." Darian says looking over at me as he spins the steering wheel with one hand. My chest flutters.

"They will?" I question looking at him, a hint of pessimism in my voice.

My blood surges with anticipation as I smile as he replies, " Hell, yeah, they will.".

"Okay remember, we are in love!" Darian says sounding stressed as he pulls up outside the house.

"Oh please, I could do this shit in my sleep." I mumble to myself getting out of the car as Darian gets out his side and walks over to me.

He asked sincerely, not understanding my confidence, "What did you say?".

"I said I would try my best!" I say smiling a cheeky grin.

He opens the door to the house and ushers me inside. I don't question that we didn't knock, instead I simply follow his instructions.

As soon as I'm in the kitchen I'm hit with the sound of tumultuous music blasting out a heavy set of Samsung speakers perched in the corner of the kitchen.

In a voice laced with concern, Darian asks me as he leans into me."are you okay?" I look up at him and nod.

"Yeah, I'm alright." I murmur unsure of how true that answer was. I will know after a couple of drinks.

I'm standing on my own by the table as Darian gets me a drink. I see Seth walking over to me glaring.

"Shit, shit triple shit!" I muttered.

"Get real I wouldn't come to a party, or is it you wouldn't want to come with me?" Seth snaps as I shake my head.

"It's not like that Seth I promise I hate shit like this you know I do, but I had to Darian made me!" I say as he laughs sardonically.

"So, Darian's your owner now, well good luck being fed puppy chow mix left over from Erin!" He says as I narrow my eyes.

"Fuck you and your holier-than-thou behavior. When have you ever told Darian you love him? I maybe eating left over chow mix but you, you aren't eating shit." I snap as he opens his mouth to say something but stops himself. He turns around and begins to walk away.

"Here, one cherry coke and vodka." Darian says as I take the drink out of his hand and down it.

"Boy, I needed that!" I say as he looks at me and raises his eyebrow.

"Right." He mumbles.

"Come on dance!" I say pulling him to Luca and his football team friends dancing in the middle of the room.

"You know, you know (you know) It's your teeth in my neck Your teeth in my neck "I sing loudly as Darian twirls me around and hands me another drink.

"What do I do it for? I've been working so hard just to
Give you more Gotta get right" I scream out the lyrics as Darian laughs.

"I'm planning to talk to Seth." I mumble as he nods.

I make my way to Seth and he turns his back on me and I tap his shoulder.

"You know I spoke about you today to Darian, he said he liked the shirt you were wearing." I say as Seth instantly turns round to face me.

"He did, say it really slowly in the exact tone he said it in." Seth says as I nod.

"Seth's t shirt it's pretty dope." I say copying Darian's mannerism as Seth squeals and I jump up and down with him.

"I'm sorry." I mumble into his ear as he nods.

"I forgive him." He shouts as I turn to him ready to argue with him about his snippy reply but stop myself.

I look over at Darian as his eyes meet mine.

As he talks, I narrow my eyes, pushing my oval glasses up my nose to see what he is saying.

You look pretty.

Even with the music blasting overhead and Luca talking to him, .

However, he still complimented me despite the over stimulating conversation.

I mouth.

Thank you.

Then he walked up to me.

"Should we get out of here? It's kind of stuffy and overrated." Darian says as I nod and follow him.

"Oh, see you round Seth it was nice seeing you." Darian says winking at Seth as Seth grows pale and starts to stutter.

"Y.... Y .... You too." Seth says waving as I giggle.

CHAPTER EIGHTEEN

"So, how'd you know Seth's in love with you?" I question sitting in the passenger side of Darian's car as he turns to me, his face suddenly pale white like a ghost.

"I didn't, but thanks for letting me know. "Darian says as my eyes widen, I glance at him dumbfounded.

"I didn't mean that I meant well he umm he is...." I start to say trying to cover up Seth's secret that I just uncovered.

"Chill I'm just messing with you; I knew it was pretty difficult not to know." He says as I giggle.

"When did you figure that out?" I ask, raising my eyebrow as Darian laughs.

"When he invited me to study in fifth grade but when I arrived at his house, he had a full face of make up on and called the studying session a date." Darian says laughing as I smile.

"He's a good guy, he deserves so much." I mumble as Darian agrees.

"He really does." Darian says smiling.

"So, where are we going? I feel a little queasy. It must be from all the vodka" I say as I watch Darian grin.

"What?" I question narrowing my eyes at him as the grin gets wider.

"I didn't give you alcohol I just had to make it look like I did" he mumbles smirking as I glare at him.

"Oh, the deceit, the betrayal" I groan slipping lower in the car seat being dramatic.

"I wasn't planning to get you drunk especially after hearing you have to watch your brother later" Darian says as I nod understanding his point.

"so, where are we going?" I ask as he smiles.

"We are en route to my favourite place" he says as he turns a corner.

"it's not the beach is it, because I have nothing against the beach it's just it's so cliche" I say as he chuckles.

"You have a very strange way of looking at things Astrid, but no, I'm not taking you to the beach.' He says as I smile.

"So where are we going then?" I ask again.

"You don't like surprises, do you?" Darian says questioning my question as I laugh.

"When all the surprises I've ever had are the people, I love leaving it's nearly impossible to find enjoyment and satisfaction in the unknown." I say as I watch his eyes flick from the road to me.

"Do you trust me?" He questions and I nod without hesitation.

"Yeah, I do." I mumble as he smiles.

"Then sit back and enjoy the journey." He says turning up the music on the car speaker.

I got everything I need
Time and space to think and breathe
What does it mean?
When cash grows on trees
Exist in superposition
Life's all about contradiction
Yin and yang
Fluidity and things

"You like Daniel Caesar?" I ask, easing the furrow in my eyebrow as he nods.

"What?" He asks as I look at him.

"I don't know I just didn't peg you as a chilled vibes kind of guy. More rock music." I say as he smirks.

"Well, I'm sorry to disappoint." He says, I shake my head.

"You haven't disappointed me, you just shocked me that's all." I say smiling.

"Not quite the stereotype you expected." Darian says smirking as I nod.

"Not quite, at all." I mumble as he stops the car.

"Where are we?" I question as he gets out first and walks over to my side of the car to let me out. I stay by his side as it's dark.

"You'll see." He says as I look at him puzzled.

I trudge through the ice-covered leaves on the ground. I almost slip a couple of times but Darian grabs onto my hand to stop me falling.

"What is this?" I question standing in what looks like a warehouse looking at a wood made box.

"You said since the funeral you've been struggling to express emotions, right?" Darian says as I nod.

"I did." 'I mumble remembering the monstrosity of a speech I gave.

He leans into a box and pulls out a hand full of fine china plates.

"When I got out of rehab I had so much hate and pent-up anger and resentment I didn't know where to put it so I came here and built this, it's my anger room." He says as I look up at him.

"You've been to rehab?" I ask as he nods and a pang of guilt hits me.

"It was two years ago I was twenty and off my head on coke twenty-four seven so my father wanted me to get my shit together for myself and my mum." He mumbles.

"But this summer you were snorting something." I say quietly as he looks down at me.

"My mother had died. I knew her chemo was rejecting but I thought I had more time with her." He mumbles.

"That's why you act like you don't care, because you really do, you really do care." I say looking at him as he chuckles deeply.

"I care too much Astrid, about everything." He says as I look at him.

"I think too much, about everything." I murmur as he smiles down at me.

"It's time to get mad but don't think." He says handing me a plate as I look down at it.

I shut my eyes imagining Susan's stupid condescending family breaking home wrecking face telling me she's sorry for my loss.

I hold the plate in my hand and fling it as hard as I can. The plate smashes into pieces as it hits the wooden wall. Suddenly, my cheeks are flushed with joy.

"You did it." Darian says smiling at me.

"I did it." I say quietly then I say it again a tiny bit louder. I walk up to Darian and jump up and down holding his hands.

"I did it, Darian I did it!" I say as he smiles widely.

"You think that's good, watch this trick shot!" He says as I watch him do a spin with the plate in his hand and he throws it hard as he smashes it into tiny fragment of pieces.

"Oh, ouch shit!" I groan.

"What, Astrid what's wrong?" Darian says walking up to me with concern on his face.

"You just got glass in my eyes OUCH!" I moan as he holds onto me.

"I'm sorry fuck I should get you to the hospit..." he starts to say as a smile crawls up my face.

"Got Ya, ha in your face, talk about a trick shot!" I shout, jumping up and down as he laughs.

CHAPTER NINETEEN

"You can come in; it's just going to be me, and Bear sleeping upstairs!" I mumble getting out Darian's car as he nods and gets out his side mum rushes out the house.

"Be safe sweetie don't answer the door to strangers!" Mum says kissing my cheek as she moves over to Darian. She holds his cheeks in her hands.

"Good man, bringing my baby home on time!" She says as Darian nods and I smile.

As soon as we get inside, I hear a bear start to cry.

"Would you excuse me a second, you can help yourself to a drink or something to eat." I mumble as Darian smiles.

I run upstairs to bear's room as he lays in bed with tears in his eyes.

"What's wrong bear?" I question as he looks at me.

"I had a dream the, the, the grinch took Christmas away." Bear says stuttering.

"Oh, bear come with me." I say holding him as we walk out of the bedroom and down the stairs.

"Hey, bear!" Darian says in a squeaky tone as I start to laugh.

"He had a nightmare that Christmas wasn't able to come because the grinch stole it so I figured we could rectify the situation for him." I say smiling.

"Okay, so what do we do? "Darian questions as I smile.

"We put the Christmas decorations up!" I say as he high-fives me as I look at my hand confused.

"What, I love Christmas." Darian says shrugging as I laughed.

"Okay so you stay with Bear while I get the tree and decorations from the boxes under the stairs." I say as Darian nods.

After about five trips back and forth from under the stairs all the Christmas decorations are stacked messily in the living room.

"Okay how about we put on some Christmas music?" I request as Bear jumps up and down in approval.

"Yay, yay Christmas is back!" Bear sings as I walk into the kitchen to get my speaker whilst Bear sits on the sofa with a ball ball in his hand.

"What you are doing for bear, it's sweet." Darian says following me into the kitchen.

"Did I just hear a compliment escape your mouth?" I mused, smirking.

With a blush of color spreading across my cheeks, I say thank you.

"Quick let's get back to bear before he eats all the tinsel." I say grabbing the speaker off the kitchen counter as Darian laughs and follows me out the kitchen.

"Who's Ready to get Christmassy?" Darian shouts as bear gets excited and starts jumping up and down on the sofa shouting me, me, me.

"Let's do this!" I say pulling out the decorations from one of the boxes whilst bear plays with the tinsel and Darian stands there looking lost. I sing Last Christmas by Wham.

An hour later.

"Hey, Darian! "I call getting his attention, he turns around and faces me as I throw a plastic ball ball at his face and it comes flying past him.

"Hey no fair, I wasn't ready!" He calls picking up the ball ball and throwing it back at me as it hits my cheek and I lean over doing a belly laugh.

"Okay, okay ready, Christmas time mistletoe and wine, Darian pissing me off all the time!" I sing loudly as Darian rugby tackles me onto the carpet and bear screams get her, get her with excitement!

"What'd you say?" Darian asks me, holding my hands above my head as I sigh in submission.

"Nothing, nothing" I murmur.

"Douche bag." I mumble as he leans down and roughly licks my cheek. My face flushes and Bear squeals with excitement.

"Did you really just lick me?" I question glaring at him as he smirks.

"A gentleman never tells." He says with a smirk.

"I will let you know when I see one." I mumble cockily as he leans down again and repeatedly licks my cheek.

"Okay, Okay I surrender." I say as he smiles.

"I knew it, I won!" He says sitting up on his knees doing a brief happy dance as I spring up and jump on his back.

I lean into him as he leans his head back into me. I turn his head to the side and give him a slobbery lick right to the cheek.

I get off his back and run into the kitchen as fast as I can.

"See who's the winner now!" I shout trying to sound manly as I laugh.

Darian runs after me catching up quickly. He grabs me picking me up and holding me by the legs. He puts me down on the counter. He stands over me close enough for me to smell the sweet smell of Pepsi on his breath.

He leans closer and I shut my eyes.

"I've never been kissed." I murmur, embarrassed. I quickly shove my hands in front of my face in fear of sounding stupid.

"But you are nineteen." He says looking shocked as I laugh a few times.

"Twenty in May." I mumble as he smiles down at me.

"Well, let me rectify the situation." Darian mumbles leaning down close to me. I shut my eyes feeling my pulse quicken.

I feel his hand cup my cheek. My heart flutters abruptly and I feel soft smooth lips pillowing mine. I've never experienced lips pillow mine before. He starts to slowly move and I imitate his movements as he pulls me closer to him by the waist. I open my eyes and look up at him. Holding the back of his neck, I move my hands.

I feel sparks like I've always imagined just not with him, but the universe has a funny way of fucking up a person's vision of perfection. This isn't what I imagined but none the less, it is perfect.

We both pull away a moment later. My attempt to get down the counter fails miserably, and I crumble to the ground. I hear Darian snigger and I glare up at him. He takes my hand in his without saying a word. We make our way to the front room seeing the perfectly decorated house.

Bear is asleep on the sofa snoring so I sit next to him and Darian joins me. I lean my head on his shoulder quietly and he strokes my hair peacefully.

CHAPTER TWENTY

"Astrid, get up, Astrid!" Someone calls as I flutter my eyes open and look up to see my mother standing over me.

Boy does this feel like Deja vu.

I look to the side of me to see Bear, I smile small then look to my other side to see Darian with his head on my shoulder. There is a line of dribble falling lower and lower from his mouth with each loud anger inducing snore that escapes his lips.

I groan and shove him off me. He falls to the floor with a thud and a small chuckle escapes my mother's lips.

"Ugh, who pushed me?" Darian says as my mother points to me and I point to her.

"Me! "Bear says suddenly jumping up from his sleep as I laugh.

"Not polite." Darian says scowling at me, knowing it was me.

"Oops." I mumble.

"Darian your dad is looking for you, he's got another work trip. You need to stop by and see him before he leaves." My mother says as Darian nods.

"I will see you out." I mutter getting up and rubbing any sleep I have, out of my eyes.

We make our way outside. I stand playing with my hands in my lap feeling nervous. I've never felt nervous about a guy before.

"I will text you okay, I had fun last night." Darian mumbles looking nervous as I nod in agreement, internally wondering what part he found fun the Christmas decorating or kissing me.

"Yes, me too." I say feeling small. He steps forward closer to me as my breath shortens. He leans down and plants a tiny kiss on my lips.

"See you round, Astrid." He whispers as he walks towards his house. I stand still on the step watching him walk away, feeling a strange sadness over his absence I've never felt before.

"I'm glad you and Darian have been getting along, but don't forget your other friends. What about Audrey? I haven't seen her here for a while. "My mother announces as soon as I get through the front door.

"Me and Audrey as well, she's just visiting her grandma. I'm pretty sure she gets back Monday Tho!" I say remembering what she said on FaceTime to me the other day.

"That's great sweetie." My mother says and before she has a chance to say anything else I speak up.

"I think I'm going to take Bear to the mall." I say as my mother smiles.

"That would be nice, I haven't gotten any sleep since my night shift two nights ago." My mother announces sounding exhausted.

An hour later.

Me and Seth are sitting in the ball pit at the local mall with bear.

"So, he kissed me." I mumble as Seth's eyes go wide.

"How was it?" He questions with an excited sparkle in his eyes, anticipating all the juicy details.

"Umm nothing like I expected, but in a pleasant way." I say as a wide grin makes its way to his face.

"So, you aren't mad at me anymore?" I question as he shakes his head abruptly.

"No, I can't have him but if anyone should be with him, I'm glad it's you." Seth says smiling as bear throws a plastic ball at Seth.

"But if you two get married and he gets bored of you and wants to explore his sexuality I will be here for his journey of gay discovery!" Seth says doing a dramatic jazz hand motion.

"Oooo, smart plan." I say sarcastically as Seth smirks

"Right." Seth says winking at me.

"So, how'd you feel about Audrey coming back Monday?" I ask looking at Seth.

"Super excited because we are throwing her a welcome home meal talking of you should probably invite your fake boy toy." Seth says as I nod.

"I will try. I'm not sure if he'd want to come, I don't think that's really his thing." I say as he smirks at me.

"Oh, so you know what his thing is?" He speaks.

"Yes, at the moment it's what he likes to call specs." I say feeling a feeling that I've never felt before.

I feel wanted.

A couple hours later

DEAR FUCKED UP THOUGHT VENT

Someone wants me.

I've never felt wanted before. Sometimes needed by my mother to watch Bear or clean the house but never wanted.

Me and Eli never really got on growing up. He saw things with rose-coloured glasses on and me well I was as cynical as I could get.

Everything I experienced was negative. My birthday, Christmas, Easter, the school nativity were all bullshit excuses to be happy.

I couldn't help it I wasn't always that way.

My father made me have a warped tainted way of looking at everything.

I thought my life was a fairy tale until he started cheating on mum. Then everything I thought was right, amazing and real was suddenly fake and broken.

But this, this doesn't feel so dark.

It feels light and fun but never fails to make my heart beat a million miles per second.

It's a strange confusing new feeling, but I like it.

CHAPTER TWENTY ONE

"So, Darian would you maybe if you want to would like to come with me to Aubrey's surprise dinner party as my plus one?" I ask looking at Seth as he shakes his head.

"God Astrid, I need more confidence from you now try again!" Seth says like a stern father as I roll my eyes.

"Darian I was thinking you could be my plus one for Audrey's surprise dinner party.

"That's my girl." Seth says while we sit on the sofa at my house and watch reruns of vampire diaries.

"Okay, okay turn it over and over and hide, he's coming." I mumble as I look down at the text he sent me. Seth jumps up off the sofa and turns the tv off. He runs up the stairs as I open the front door.

"Hey." I say looking at Darian as he starts and plays with his messy black hair.

"I wanted to talk to you." Darian mumbles as I look at him and notice how nervous he is.

"What is it, Darian?" I question as he looks down at the floor.

"The kiss, I shouldn't have kissed you it was, well it was a mistake." He murmurs as I look down at my feet feeling the rejection that I knew was coming but naïvely hoped wouldn't.

"Right the kiss I forgot about that; I didn't think it was that big of a deal." I say shrugging playing it cool.

"Okay as long as this hasn't made the agreement weird, we are pretending and I just don't want to ruin our plan." Darian says as I laugh.

"Geez dude that kiss is really living rent free in your mind. (Actually, mine but he won't ever know.)" I say trying to play it cool as he laughs.

"So do you want to be my plus one at Audrey's welcome home dinner Monday night?" I ask as he nods.

"I can do that." He says as I feel the awkward tension creeping up.

"If that's all, I will text you Monday." I say as he turns around and walks out. I shut the front door and sigh as Seth walks down the stairs.

"Don't, say a word!" I hiss out as Seth smirks.

"Maybe I do have a chance with him." Seth says doing a miniature model strut.

"It's okay baby men suck." Seth says walking up to me stroking my hair like I'm a dog.

"Thanks, but it's not that big a deal." I say while lying through my teeth.

"Right." Seth says clearly unconvinced.

A couple hours later.

DEAR FUCKED UP THOUGHT VENT

I'm back to day one.

And it's kind of comforting to me that I feel fine about Darian regretting the kiss.

If I cared I would be a little bit pissed that he stole my first kiss without asking. In addition, he had the nerve to take it back but seeing as I don't care, I'm not.

My phone starts to ring, I put my journal down picking up my phone noticing it's an unknown number.

"Hello?" I say down the phone feeling a twinge of anxiety that I get whenever an unknown number calls me.

"Hi, is this Astrid I'm violet." The girl says.

Violet, do I know you?" I replied.

"No, I was hooking up with a guy I met at a frat party a couple weeks ago. And well he took me back to his room on campus and now he's crying about his dad being dead and he's really drunk and I don't know what to do." She mumbles as I sigh.

"It's Eli, isn't it?" I question rolling my eyes.

"Yes." She says straight away.

"Send me the address and I will be there as soon as I can." I say then put the phone down.

It's half twelve

Mum is at work and Bear is in bed. I can't wake him.

Fuck.

I dial Darian's number.

After a second he picks up.

"Darian something has happened and I need you to drive me somewhere." I mumble hoping he will say yes.

"What the hell Astrid it's midnight and I was asleep!" He snaps as I sigh.

"It's not for me it's for Eli." I say hoping he will say yes now.

"what's wrong with him?" Darian questions suddenly sounding awake, God forbid he shows care for me.

"he's freaking out about dad in front of some girl" I mumble.

"Is she hot?" Darian suddenly asks, testing my last nerve.

"Darian, please stick to the situation!" I said anxiously.

"Fine, fine I will be outside in ten be ready" he says bluntly and puts down the phone without a mutter of a goodbye.

Why does he seem so pissed at me? He was the one who said he regretted the kiss.

I just played along.

I get dressed into some black leggings and a vintage Disney t shirt that's two sizes too big.

I run out of my bedroom and pick up Bear, wrap him in his blanket, and rock him to sleep as he starts to wake up.

I walk downstairs being careful not to fall. I grab my handbag and walk out the front door. I see Darian standing by his car.

"Why are you bringing Bear with you?" Darian asks.

"Mums at work." I say quietly as he avoids eye contact with me.

"If you give him to me, my dad can watch him and will get text updates to your mum." Darian says as I nod and hand Bear to Darian.

He walks into his house quietly and then a second later walks out alone.

"How come your dad's up?" I inquire.

"He just got home from work." Darian says not bothering to look at me as we get in the car.

We start the drive to ELAC and it's completely silent.

"Just so you know I'm doing this for Eli not you!" Darian remarks.

Oh, we are back to hating each other, I guess.

"That's fine." I mumble as he continues looking at the road.

I notice a girl with a short black Bob hair cut standing at the entrance of our destination after a long silent awkward thirty-minute drive.

Astrid, your brother is in there." The girl said standing at the door.

Darian walks past me and straight into the room.

"Eli, you okay?" I hear Darian say as I sigh and walk in.

"What the hell is she doing here?" Eli snaps and I chuckle lightly.

"It's nice to see you too, bro!" I murmur as he glares at me.

"Why are you here, it's all your fault, you told mum about dad cheating again we could've been happy you always ruin everything" he says crying and cradling himself on the bed.

"I know I suck I ruin everything. If I didn't exist dad would still be alive mum would still be married, and you would be happy." I mumble out feeling self-hatred.

"Yep, for once you are right." He hisses out.

"Why did you ask for me Eli?" I asked.

Because I have no one else, I quit my job at the tech shop and I am about to be homeless. I can no longer afford to live here unless I beg to go back." He says, sobbing harder.

"So, come home." I say as he nods.

"Fine." He says and wipes his eyes but then starts to cry harder.

"You're drunk you need to sleep." I say as he shakes his head then hugs me.

"I'm sorry I hate you so much I don't want to, I just, I miss dad." He says crying as I stroke his head.

"It's fine Eli." I mumble as Darian walks with Eli to the car and I grab Eli's gym bag getting him some clothes and his wallet.

"Thanks for telling us violet that was thoughtful of you." I say smiling at the girl.

"I really care about him." She says as I smile.

"Well thanks, again." I say walking away from her making my way to the car.

I get in the back next to Eli and he lays his lips flat against the window as I can't help but chuckle.

We are half way through the drive home when Eli mutters something.

"I wish you were never born."

I look in the rear-view mirror and see Darian looking at me.

"Yeah, me too buddy," I murmur looking down at the floor.

As Darian's hand makes its way around the car seat, I look up to see his hand on top of mine as he strokes it.

I hold it in my hand for a second then he pulls it back putting it back on the steering wheel.

Every now and then I notice his eyes dart from the road to me in the mirror.

That is until I fall asleep.

CHAPTER TWENTY TWO

"Astrid we are back." Darian says tapping me as I sit up and slyly wipe away any dribble from my mouth.

"Where's Eli?" I questioned.

"My dad thought it was wise if he slept at ours tonight, he didn't want Eli drunk around Bear, Bears with your mum." Darian says.

Where is Eli, I mean whose room is he in?" I ask.

"he's asleep snoring in my bed." Darian says as I chuckle.

"You can stay with us if you like, I mean the spare room." I say as he nods.

As I get out of his car, slam the door and start running to catch up to him, he says, "Thank you." Nodding, he starts walking towards the house.

"Why were you so cold to me?" I ask as he stops walking.

"Darian?" I say quietly as he looks down at me.

"You said the kiss wasn't a big deal and you'd forgotten about it." Darian says as I laugh and he raises his eyebrow at me.

"Because, you said it was a mistake, am I supposed to enjoy a mistake Darian? It tasted bittersweet!" I say as he shakes his head.

"No, I didn't mean it was a mistake. I just, I don't want to lead you on." He says as I glare at him.

"Darian, I'm not a little kid I can feel what I want to feel." I say crossing my arms like a silly kid.

Having said that, what was the kiss to you and what did it mean for you, on three and two?" He begins to ask.

"One"

"Fun!" He speaks

I murmur, "You have feelings, I mean fun!".

"What?" He asks, and I thank God that he couldn't hear what I said.

"I said fun!" I say, smiling a false innocent smile.

"Okay well, so we got that sorted." He says as i nod.

"Fab!" He says smiling.

"That's fine." I mumble.

"Good." He says smirking.

"Great!" I say glaring at him as he pulls me in by the waist and wraps his arms around me.

He leans down and presses his lips to mine; I follow along I press my hand to his jaw and kiss back sweetly. He stops kissing and leans his forehead on mine.

"Let's go to bed." He says holding onto my hand and leading me to the house as I nod.

The second we get through the door his lips are on mine as he pushes me against the front door and I kiss back.

He pulls my top over my head dropping it to the floor revealing my bare torso.

He kisses down to my bra then back up to my mouth.

He pulls me up the stairs to my room not letting go of me. The second my bedroom door is shut he turns me around so my back is backed up against the wall. He kisses me so passionately it knocks the wind out of me.

He pulls his t-shirt off as I look at his torso. I run my fingers up and down his toned stomach and I walk to the bed as he follows.

"Only you." I mumble quietly.

"What, Astrid?" Darian asked me as he held me close to him.

"I'd only do this, only for you." I say looking up at him.

"You are a virgin, aren't you?" He questions as I nod.

"I knew it!" He says smirking as I push his shoulder playfully and he chuckles.

"Lay with me." He says as I nod and lay back as he does.

"You think my mum made it to heaven?" Darian asks looking up at my ceiling as I nod.

"Definitely, you think my dad made it to heaven?" I ask and he chuckles.

"No, there's no way." Darian says as I laugh sardonically.

"Yeah, me too. He's probably in hell cheating on Susan." I say smirking as the thought dances in my mind.

"You think if you died, you'd make it to heaven?" Darian asks and I shake my head.

"What?" I mumble as he glares at me.

"We are being honest, aren't we?" I ask as he nods his head.

"I don't think I'd go to heaven my thoughts are too offensive. I've screwed up too many times for god to let me in the magic gates in the sky." I say as Darian laughs.

"Meet me in hell?" Darian gestures for me to shake his hand.

"Meet you there." I say smiling, shaking his hand.

He leans onto his side and I copy.

He holds onto my jaw. "I've wanted you to be mine for so long." He muttered, my eyes turn bright and wide.

"You've wanted me?" I ask as a tear slips down my face and he wipes it away.

"More than anything," He says. I wrap my arms around his torso, and he holds me tightly. I burrow my face deep into his neck.

I spread a few kisses up and down his neck, I look up at him and he smiles.

"Your mine, you've been mine, you will always be mine, no one knows you like I do my love." He says as I open my mouth shocked, he takes the chance to close my mouth by inclosing it with his lips.

The kiss deepens and he pulls his grey joggers off along with my black leggings.

"Are you sure you want this?" He questions as I nod.

"More than anything." I say holding his jaw, he leans down and kisses me.

CHAPTER TWENTY THREE

He starts to pull down my grey boring underwear, spreading sweet small kisses down my thigh.

"Ready?" Darian asks leaning up on his elbows and smiling.

"Yea." I murmur feeling a-little scared and afraid.

I mean who wouldn't be? It's my first time okay, I'm fricking scared.

He leans down slowly and kisses me distracting me from the pulsing between my legs. His area is tight against me.

I feel a sting of pain rise up through my lower half up to my stomach. I push my head back against the pillow as he enters me. Thick beads of sweat float from my forehead down to my neck.

"Are you okay?" Darian asks through heavy breaths. I nod slowly unsure if I am okay, it feels strange.

I tell him to keep moving. He doesn't hesitate and pushes on. I wince in pain as I indent my nails deep into his back. He growls against my ear as I feel a tingle go up and down my spine.

"You are so fucking sexy." He groans looking down at me, his dark hair floating above me, as he grips onto my right breast whilst thrusting deeper into me then back out again, my cheeks tint a few shades deeper into a deep beetroot colour.

I moan out arching my back like a cat, feeling his fingers skim down my stomach sloppily. Things feel better and the pain subsides fast as a scream erupts from my throat. It's muffled by the sweet taste of Darian's lips attached to mine.

The headboard bangs louder against the wall louder with each thrust of Darian's hips.

"Oh, God!" I cry out, jerking into Darian again and again feeling deep euphoria.

"We need to stop." Darian mumbles as I come down from my sudden explosion of butterflies deep, deep down.

"Why?" I ask kissing behind his ears. He continues to thrust faster.

"I'm not wearing protection." He says as I groan.

"Fuck." I hiss rolling my eyes back as Darian watches and grows stiff.

A deep groan spills out of his mouth and I rise up quickly, him holding me still.

"Did you, just? "I question going still.

"I didn't mean to; fuck the way you rolled your eyes." He mumbles as I look at him my cheeks crimson red, hair stuck to my cheeks with the residue of sweat.

"I need to pee." I say getting up trying to stand but failing miserably.

He gets up and pulls his boxers and jeans on, saying, "I can help you stay there.".

He walks over to my side helping me up and walking me to the restroom.

"I'm going to wait in your room." He says as I nod before I have a chance to shut the door. Holding his hand in the way, he takes my lips in his and gives me a breathy kiss.

After peeing and splashing my face with water I take a slow walk to my room.

The bedroom doors shut. I push the door open and notice Darian's not there.

Panic fills me and I run to my window ignoring the aching between my thighs.

I pull my curtains open seeing Darian's car speed down the road.

Tears escape my eyes, as I wipe them furiously feeling ashamed of myself.

I walk to the bathroom turning on the shower, I walk back to my room stripping my blood-stained sheets. I can still smell Darian on my pillow as I fling it across the room.

I walk back into the bathroom as I shove the dirty sheets into the laundry bin and peel my clothes off my sweaty body. I step into the shower staying still and just letting the water pour off me in small droplets.

I use half a bottle of vanilla and coconut shower gel in a sly attempt at getting the feel of his touch off me.

But no use, the memory of what just happened will be
Indented in my brain until I am no longer alive.

The way he kissed me I can still feel it.

I run my fingers over my lips and rub at my bottom lip in an angry sloppy attempt to erase the feel of his lips on mine.

Hold onto my hips remembering how he lifted them thrusting deeper.

I bite back my bottom lip as I cradle my body in my arms.

A soothing, sad, self-comfort I've had since I was small and craved pity or comfort, but was never given it.

Tomorrow is the last day of classes before Christmas. This is the day that I was planning to host a welcome home party for Audrey. At that party me and Darian would show up like a couple, kiss like a couple. This is because we just made love like people, people who are in love. Then he left me like I meant nothing to him.

I was conquering, that's all I was.

I should've known he told me what we were, we were fun that's all, so why did it feel like more, why did my heart tell me it was more.

CHAPTER TWENTY FOUR

It's true to most that lying in bed is a waste of time, no productive qualities at all, but when ninety percent of day to day living activities have the chance of pain or even sudden death, to be pain or death free seems, simply the most appealing and appropriate of things for me to do.

I roll over deeper into my clean sheets hugging my duvet to my body feeling the cold cling to me, even though the windows aren't open in my house.

I made some bullshit excuse to mum. I told her I was sick and couldn't move. Feeling sick made my excuse sound like a profound prophecy. My stomach is empty, I haven't eaten since lunch yesterday, and I can't move. I've tried to get up, but it feels like the bed has a hold on me. I'm safe here, I'm wanted here.

My sweet depressing comfort is disturbed by a sudden loud knock on the front door.

I ignore it, hoping that it will die down and whoever is will go away.

But no, the knocking continues and only gets louder.

I shut my eyes and continue to ignore it. My phone starts to buzz and I look to see who is calling.

Seth.

I couldn't bear to face Seth right now. I can only imagine the unimaginable embarrassment of telling him I lost my virginity. This was to someone who used me for what a regular person would call a quick fuck but what I would call a time passer.

Small rocks start to fly at my window hitting them loudly, but I ignore them, knowing it's Seth.

Eli went back to college this morning and also back to hating me, what else could one expect?

I haven't heard from Darian, I mean why would I? It's just human nature, people use people, that's just the reason for living. Back in the old days people used people all the time. These days it's more stigmatised and frowned upon but it simply happens and you have to get over it or you give up. I opt for option two. It's easier that way.

I ignore my phone and the door and eventually they both become silent.

DEAR FUCKED UP THOUGHT VENT

Do you know what sucks about childhood abandonment? Not the abandonment part that's for sure, but the part where you discover it's your fault, the part where you realise people are leaving you not because they are the problem, but because you are, not because you're not enough or because you're a terrible person or because they don't like the way you think, no it's none of them, the fact is its because you are you and that's what they don't want.

Do you know what also sucks about childhood abandonment? The disgusting stench of desperation for intimacy that follows you around, it doesn't matter what kind of intimacy, just that you want to be wanted. No matter how hard you try to shake it away, it stays with you. Like a stray dog that you feed at the local park. It followed you home, eventually you can't get rid of it, so you keep it and keep it with you until someone actually wants you or until the alternative,

You end up alone.

A fear that has been around since birth. I don't know what's so scary about being alone. I kind of like it. The sense that I can truly be myself by myself. However, it also scares me. I can't be around anybody else without offending them or them finding me completely and utterly bonkers. Not in a pleasant way.

It's not that I don't want to be friends with Seth or Audrey. It's that they don't really know me, and I'm afraid that if they did, they'd leave me. That's why ever since I was seven, I've kept this silly little fucked up thought vent. It never judged me, never told me I was strange or cynical. It told me that I could open up without outside opinions influencing my thought process.

I was completely content with shoving my feelings and thoughts down into this small book that was before, before I met him and everything changed.

CHAPTER TWENTY FIVE

It's the morning of New Year's Eve

I haven't seen Darien since that night. I can't say that I'm disappointed. Things are exactly how they were designed to be. He was supposed to leave me and I was supposed to be alone. My brother is supposed to hate me and my mother is supposed to work twenty-four seven. Most of the time that I spend is watching my younger brother.

Everything is exactly how it should be in the world.

I had my period a week ago. If I'm being honest, I'm glad I'm not having a child. It didn't really cross my mind. Nothing seemed to have crossed my mind these past few weeks.

Maybe it's because I'm on new anxiety meds that make me feel like a zombie. The things I worry about regularly, I don't care about at all, but when the meds wear off, I worry about complete irrelevant things such as when I was cooking banana bread and burned it, I cried for three hours after or when I was watching bear and we ran out of juice I felt so guilty I thought about it for so long then I cried for an hour.

Mum and Joe have been hanging out again. I'm happy she's not alone, I'd never want her to feel alone.

I run downstairs to answer the front door. I look in front of me to see Seth and Audrey standing with a make-up bag a dress and some heels in their hands.

I look behind them and see Erin making her way into Darian's home.

I nod slowly as Seth looks at me like I'm crazy.

"You are actually agreeing to this?" Seth says as Audrey looks at me a little dumbfounded.

"Yes of course I am, what am I doing again?" I mumbled, as Seth faked a face palm and Audrey giggled.

"You are coming with us to the New Year's party at Jones house" Audrey exclaims getting excited. It's safe to say they both forgave me for skipping Audrey's welcome home party.

"Yes, I mean no why would I do that." I say as I watch through Darian's window like a peeping tom, Erin starts to kiss Darian passionately.

I feel my heart sink.

Come on!, they have to do it when my anxiety meds are wearing off.

Seth looks behind me to see what I'm looking at.

"I guess the deal with you guys is off." Seth states as Audrey looks where Seth is looking.

"I guess it is." I say shrugging.

As she gently holds my arm, she says, "Oh babe.".

"It's fine, it's not like it was real, it was just an unauthentic arrangement." I say shrugging putting on the persona of someone who doesn't care.

But I do care, I care too much.

"So, the party." Seth says wiggling his eyebrows, as I sigh.

"What about it?" I ask, narrowing my eyes at him. It's not really a priority for me, it's never been.

I did however manage to get a job. My mother's work friend owns the local library. She interviewed me the other day and I will start January 3rd!

Books are my favorite thing. I sort the books read to the kids every day and also work at the checkout.

"Hello, earth to Astrid!" Audrey says waving her hand in front of my face.

"Yes, let's get dressed together!" I say smiling remembering it's a new year and I am a new me, as cliché it sounds.

We are upstairs in my bedroom with old school Whitney Houston playing when there's a knock at my bedroom door.

"Yeah?" I say opening my bedroom door as Eli walks into my room. His eyes instantly stop on Audrey. I turn to look at her seeing the crimson colour on her cheeks.

"I was wondering if you wanted me to watch Bear tonight so you can stay out a little longer you've been watching him all week. "Eli says smiling softly at me, as I shake my head.

"You only got back from college yesterday, surely you must be tired!" I say as Audrey looks at us.

"Well, you know I'm actually not feeling very well, you know, cramps" Audrey says leaning over and holding her stomach as Seth raises his eyebrow at her.

"You could always keep me company, we could watch a movie, hang" Eli says sounding nervous.

"Audrey, I thought this was the biggest party of the year "Seth says as I can't help but smirk and giggle.

"Actually, it isn't the biggest party of the year, it's the last, I'm just not feeling it" Audrey says shrugging.

"Okay well, we understand and like Eli said you should stay here with him and bear" I say smiling as Eli's eyes go wide.

" I mean, if, only if you want too" Eli mumbles and Audrey nods.

"I'd love too, but pizzas on you!" Audrey says as I smile. I love her dominating personality. She knows what she wants when she wants it and most of the time, she gets it.

"Okay deal!" Eli says without a second thought.

Eli walks out of the room and back into his room.

"You are planning to help us pick an outfit though, aren't you?" I ask as Audrey raises her eyebrow.

"Do you even have to ask? You've just given me free rein to style you, and you think I'd say no" Audrey says as I laugh.

"Nope, I was just double checking. "I say giggling as God is a woman by Ariana Grande comes on and Seth turns it up singing loudly.

"My one, it lingers when we're done, you'll believe God is a woman" Seth sings doing jazz hands as Audrey twirls.

I giggle and hold a pretty dark green skater dress up to my body.

"This is what I want to wear, this" I say smiling as Seth nods.

"This is perfect" Audrey says smirking.

CHAPTER TWENTY SIX

I hold onto Seths arm as I get out his car, attempting to walk in the sand-coloured Gucci espadrille wedges Audrey lent me it's not working so well since I've almost just tripped up the curb.

"My ankles hurt! "I say complaining to Seth as he laughs.

"Just take them off, I won't tell Audrey!" Seth says as I look up at him and raise my eyebrow.

"Why are you being so kind to me? Normally you'd tell me to grow some balls and get on with it.

"On the contrary, I can actually be kind, sometimes." Seth says as I laugh.

"Ready?" Seth asked, getting ready to walk into Jones' house.

"I think so." I mumble.

"Too late to turn back now, grow some balls and get your ass in there!" Seth says, reverting to normal Seth.

"That's the Seth I know and love." I say smiling up at him. I follow him into the house, where I am hit by the smell of spiced wine.

"Hey Jones, what's with the Christmas drinks?" I ask as Jones laughs.

"Oh that, yeah my mum made some spiced red wine punch on Christmas Day. My dad wasn't a fan so I told her I'd drink it, with help from you guys." He says smiling as I laugh.

"Well what kind of person would I be to not try your mum's punch!" I say laughing.

"A terrible one." He says handing me a red Solo cup full of red wine spiced punch.

I put it to my lips and swallowed it.

I give Jones a wide smile and walk around him to the bin dropping the cup in.

I start walking in the hallway looking for Seth when I see Darian walk in with some guy standing next to him.

I stop dead still and look at him.

The song playing is "Poison" by Rita Ora and I know for a fact Seth put the song on to annoy me.

My eyes are glued to him, as I see Erin grab his hand. It's as if the music stopped, the people stopped chatting, and the other sounds stopped.

Suddenly, I look away ripping myself from his gaze. I run up the stairs and open the door to the bathroom, storming in.

"Oh my god, I'm so sorry I'm just going to umm, yeah bye." I say getting awkward as a couple I know from college are practically ripping each other's clothes off and chewing on each other's faces.

They didn't even bother to look round or stop, I just slammed the door and walked to the room with the large bathroom sign on the door. I open the bathroom door and shut it feeling stupid.

The bathroom door opens and Darian steps inside.

"No, I'm not doing this here, not now!" I snap as he shakes his head.

"You have to talk to me sometime, Astrid I found out something that night I didn't want to leave you please believe me!" Darian says pleading as I chuckle dryly.

"And why should I believe a thing that comes out of your mouth, Darian? You got what you wanted then you left me!" I mumble as he walks up to me. I step back holding onto the edge of the bath tub to prevent me from losing balance.

"It wasn't like that my dad he saw us walking in together, he rang me and told me something!" Darian says as I glare at him.

"He told you what?" I question as he shakes his head.

"I can't tell you okay, it's not my secret to tell!" Darian says as I nod.

"Fine, this conversation is terminated!" I exclaim stepping around Darian to walk out the bathroom. He grabs my arm pulling me back.

As he holds onto my arm, I look directly into his eyes. I will leave you alone if you tell me what happened didn't mean anything to you." he says. While he leans in close to my lips, I bite back my bottom lip.

"I can't do that." I said.

"Um, so that means you're saying I mean something to you." He says his breath hovers over my mouth.

"Darian, it did but did not continue beyond that. It stopped the moment I realised you used me," I told myself.

He tells me and reaches for my jaw line as he says, "You've never been a good liar; you can't keep lying and avoiding what you really feel."

"Watch me." I hissed pulling out of his grasp and walking out the bathroom.

I finally find Seth and he's completely wasted.

"What's wrong why are you so drunk? You said you weren't planning to get wasted!" I say looking at Seth.

"Jones is gay!" Seth announces loudly. I grab him shoving my hand over his mouth.

So, not only did I sleep with a womaniser but also, had a crush on a gay man.

"Shhhh, don't tell anyone!" I hiss.

"I thought I loved him but then he has to leave and get with a stupid woman!" Seth says gagging dramatically as I can't help but giggle.

"If it's any consolation I had sex with Darian!" I say sighing.

"What the fuck is wrong with us, and also how the hell is that supposed to make me feel better? You slept with my metaphorical soulmate!" Seth states crossing his arms as I roll my eyes.

"Yep, I'm the most awful person ever!" I say as Seth hits my shoulder.

"Ouch, what was that for!" I say as Seth glares at me.

"Just because you did something ethically challenging, that you are definitely planning to do again doesn't make you the worst. Geez Astrid you gotta stop thinking everything that goes wrong or happens is your fault!" Seth says as I look at him.

"Wanna get married?" I ask smirking, looking up at him as his eyes widen.

"Okay, you are pushing it, now I take back that last statement you are the most awful!" Seth says as I take my turn to hit his arm.

"Thanks Seth!" I say smiling as I hear drunk in love by Beyoncé start to play.

This was the song that was playing the first time I met Darian. I felt his eyes watch me as my hips circled slowly to the rhythm of the song back in summer.

The first time I knew he'd be something to me.

I look over at Darian as he stands with Seth drinking some sort of alcoholic drink from the red solo cup.

His eyes stay locked to mine and he mouths something.

I love you.

Is it right? My eyes are bulging, am I seeing it right? I shut my eyes then open them again hoping it was just a mistake but when I open them, there he is standing mouthing I love you over and over again.

I open my mouth and let the words escape me all the way from my heart.

I love you too.

We are both in a hurry to get to each other, so we push past drunken people who are groping each other whilst dancing.

Without a word he grabs my face pulling me in kissing me so passionately I feel all the air in my lungs drain out of me.

I pull away looking at everyone as they continue to dance.

"Let's go, let's get out of here." Darian says as I nod. He takes my hand in his as he walks out the door.

We make our way to the car. Darian slips into his seat and I get in my side. However, it doesn't take him long for him to pull me over to him and down onto his lap.

A gasp escapes me feeling him underneath me.

"Are you ready?" He whispers in my ear as I look around me at the empty street still hearing the booming music from Jones house.

"Yeah." I say as I lean in feeling brave and I kiss him feeling us together.

Before I know it, his large hands are on the bare skin of my legs. I'm lifting him up so he can take off his jeans and pull his underwear down. He rips the protection open sliding it on himself.

I pull my underwear down eagerly.

"We have to be quiet, okay?" Darian says as I nod and slowly lower myself. I instantly tense my shoulders feeling a familiar but foreign feeling in my lower stomach.

I hold onto him as I slowly move up and down feeling his legs eagerly helping me as he thrusts up.

I hold onto a chunk of his hair as he leans up grabbing my lips in his biting my bottom lip hungrily.

I let out a couple moans as Darian speeds up but his lips muffle them.

"Oh fuck, Astrid," he groans and releases my lips, and I'm thankful I can bury my head back into his shoulder to muffle my gasps.

Feeling his body heat against me. I stop mid-moan. I feel his warm breath against my neck as he brushes my hair aside with one hand. His other hand finds my waist to hold me in place as a deep groan pushes from his mouth and I feel like I'm seeing stars hitting my high.

He leans his head back on the seat and I rest my head on his chest.

A minute later I get up off him and pull my underwear up and my dress down and sit back in the seat next to him, whilst he cleans himself up.

"We should go home, it's getting dark." I say as Darian nods but I notice he's gone quiet.

"What's wrong, you aren't planning to leave me, are you?" I whispered, sounding more desperate than I wanted to sound.

"No specs, I love you." He says leaning over and planting a spot kiss on my lips.

The drive home is completely silent. A thick atmosphere surrounds the car like an impending storm.

Anxiety fills my body and I start to wonder if I should be feeling regret or enough discomfort.

As soon as we get home, Darian and I get out of the car.

"I'm going to go, I'm super tired." Darian says as I look at him in confusion. Did I say something, did I do something.

"It's nine Darian, don't beat around the bush just tell me you made another mistake I was the mistake just tell me, I can take it." I say shrugging acting like it's no big deal.

"No, it wasn't a mistake okay I just, I need to tell you something in the morning I told you I'm not leaving you now, not ever." He says holding my hand as I nod.

"Okay, we should go in. I think my brother and Audrey are watching a movie. We could hang with them and you could stay the night. "I say looking at him as we walk to the front door.

"Sounds like a plan." Darian says smiling nervously as I unlock the front door and walk in.

The house is quiet so we walk straight into the front room.

There's a large banner hanging up. It's gold with white writing on.

Darian's hand was slipping from my grasp as tears brimmed my eyes.

"What the fuck!" I say looking at Eli and Audrey holding glasses of alcohol as some people from mum's work stand around and clap. I watch my mother standing with her hand out whilst Joe, Darian's dad holds a ring to her marriage finger.

"We are getting married, Astrid!"

BOOK TWO
COMING SOON!

THANK YOU FOR
READING

Printed in Great Britain
by Amazon